Aaron

Hathaway House, Book 1

Dale Mayer

Books in This Series:

Aaron, Book 1

Brock, Book 2

AARON: HATHAWAY HOUSE, BOOK 1
Dale Mayer
Valley Publishing Ltd.

Copyright © 2019

ISBN-13: 978-1-773361-47-5
Print Edition

About This Book

Welcome to Hathaway House, a heartwarming military romance series from USA TODAY best-selling author Dale Mayer. Here you'll meet a whole new group of friends, along with a few favorite characters from Heroes for Hire. Instead of action, you'll find emotion. Instead of suspense, you'll find healing. Instead of romance, ... oh, wait. ... There is romance—of course!

Welcome to Hathaway House. Rehab Center. Safe Haven. Second chance at life and love.

Former Navy SEAL Aaron Hammond has no idea how he wound up at Hathaway House, Texas. Nor does he particularly care. All he can see is his anger. Anger at the betrayal that destroyed his physical body and at the loss of the future he wanted but that he'll never have now. He's a cripple, less than half a man, and all he can look forward to is a half life, alone with himself and his pain.

Dani Hathaway runs Hathaway House with her father, an ex-military man nicknamed the Major, and she knew Aaron and his brother SEAL Levi in another life. Levi was a good friend to her through her difficult teen years, but it was Aaron who caught her eye more than a decade ago. When she heard what happened to him, she moved heaven and earth to get him to Hathaway House, where she could help him regain his health and return him to the man he used to be.

Old feelings resurface as Dani continues to push Aaron

to acknowledge that his life is not over, and that, if he chooses, he can find both love and a future at Hathaway House.

Sign up to be notified of all Dale's releases here!

https://smarturl.it/DaleNews

Chapter 1

WHERE THE HELL am I? Aaron Hammond understood this was Texas. But he'd never seen this corner of it before. A place he couldn't have imagined. If he'd been asked to guess his location, he'd have said Kentucky, with the rolling green hills, white-fenced fields and ... horses.

Aaron reached out his hand to stop the orderly's progress. It already choked him that he couldn't manage this short distance on his own. Accepting help was one thing—charity was the worst though.

They had come from the parking lot—which was just dust and gravel, nothing even close to resembling the clean medical facility he'd left this morning. He took several deep gulps of the fresh country air and wondered what life had done to him. He'd gone from a spotless naval hospital, with daily visits to a top physical therapy department, to this. Sure, he'd been screaming and hollering to get the hell out of there. That will happen when you take an active, top-of-the-top, best-of-the-best SEAL and knock him flat—removing what was left of his leg and ripping the shit out of his back. He wasn't paralyzed, but it would be a long time before he was whole again. He could live without the leg. He didn't have much choice—he had to live without a leg—but he wanted to make sure his back was strong enough to carry the extra burden.

Unnerved by this 180 jolt to his system that had him feeling unbalanced and off-center, he went on the defensive.

"What the hell is this place?" he asked. He'd arrived by ambulance—the paperwork had been exchanged, and now he was in the care of this man who, according to the tag on his colored shirt, was named George. Aaron had ignored the earlier introductions.

"Hathaway House," George replied calmly.

What kind of name was that anyway? It sounded like a last patch of ground for aging horses. Which just might be appropriate, considering the ones he could see in the distance. "How the hell did I get here?"

"This was chosen to be the next-best step in your healing and recovery. You signed the transfer papers."

"See? I hear those words, but they don't compute." If there was one thing he liked, it was all his boxes checked—his *T*s crossed and his *I*s dotted. Not to mention he was a bit of a computer geek. None of this made any sense. He understood code, but he could decipher nothing here—just a blank slate of confusion. Sure, he'd signed transfer papers, but he'd had no idea he was coming to a place like this.

"I believe you requested a change of scenery." George pushed him up the ramp. "This is a great place."

The new deck opened out into a much better view. If this was a ranch, it was like none he'd ever seen before. It looked like a converted old school, with some kind of a Western theme. It wasn't terribly pretty, and yet it wasn't terribly institutionalized either. It had … character. He gave a half snort under his breath and settled back into the wheelchair. Instead of going through the double entry doors, George pushed Aaron around to the back of the deck and stopped, letting him take a look.

Beautiful green fields to the left, more fields to the right—a mix of horses thrown in. He wasn't exactly sure, but he thought he also saw a donkey and maybe a mule. The animals grazed happily. A picture-postcard moment. They looked happy and to be enjoying life as best they could.

His heart went out to one of the horses, an animal meant to race and run for miles, with some kind of artificial leg. How the hell did they get the horse to accept that? As he watched, a three-legged dog came running toward them, its tail wagging. Another dog came running, a set of wheels attached to its back, and barking like a crazy man.

Then Aaron understood.

This wasn't a place just for injured people, this was for injured animals too.

A heavy breath escaped his chest. As much as he hated to think he didn't belong here, a part of him said he belonged more than most. He looked down to where his leg should've been, then back at the dog with wheels. The animal didn't seem to give a damn, even missing both hind legs. That old phrase, *life is a bitch, and then you die,* ran through his head.

He'd been saying that over and over again for most of his life. But now, for the first time, he wondered what it would take to change that attitude, to be more like the dog's? He reached out a hand, wincing as this odd angle pulled on his back. The dog reached up and shoved his nose into Aaron's palm, as if he knew Aaron's range of movement was limited.

Aaron gently stroked the top of the dog's head and scratched behind his ears.

"Lots of animals are out here," George said. "The little guy with the wheels is called Racer. The three legged one is Tipler."

George pushed the wheelchair forward until they came around to the back where the deck widened again into an area that ran almost the full length and width of the house. Multiple chairs were set about, and wheelchair ramps ran up and down. At the back of the deck, parked close to a heavy wooden railing, was a very large black man, missing both legs, cuddling with the smallest dog ever.

The realization came to him that, although he was here, in a brand-new environment, nothing had changed. He was still surrounded by people as broken and defeated as he was. He made an effort to glance away from the big man and the tiny dog but not before he had caught the man's gaze.

The man studied Aaron for a moment and then gave a slow smile. "Welcome. Right now you hate it. You want to be anywhere else but here. However, in a couple weeks, you'll never want to be anywhere else."

Aaron was pretty damned sure that would never happen. He gave a curt nod before George pushed him through the open-wall space into a massive living room or community area. George pushed the chair all the way through the room, back to the front doors they'd avoided in the first place.

Once there, George stopped at the reception desk. "Dani, this is Aaron."

Aaron studied the woman who had changed the tone of George's voice. She was young but not too young. She was pretty but not too pretty. In fact, a whole lot about her was just right. Yet something was also familiar about her.

Well, that was just too damned bad. The chances of him ever having a sexual relationship again were zero. He might still have his genitals, but he hadn't seen one sign that the damned thing worked anymore. No way in hell would he start a relationship as half a man. Better if he bowed out forever. Friendships without benefits would be his new normal.

He looked up at the woman, her huge chocolate-brown eyes and the soft look in them. He'd never seen that look before, at least never turned in his direction. He gave her a curt nod. "Morning."

"Good morning, Aaron. I've been looking forward to your arrival."

Inasmuch as he wanted to say a lot about that—how he didn't want to be here, and actually why *was* he here?—the only thought in his mind currently was about losing himself in those eyes swelling with compassion. A gaze that said she knew and understood his thoughts, his turmoil, but was happy to see him anyway. A gaze that made him want to believe in a better life. That such a thing was possible—even though he already knew differently.

How sad was that?

DANI HATHAWAY HAD awaited his arrival for days, and she'd fully expected him to not recognize her. She'd hoped he would, but ... well, it had been a long time. What she hadn't expected—and should have, all things considered—was his anger.

Dani returned her attention to the paperwork in front of her before facing the computer screen to check Aaron in.

Another angry soldier. Angry at the world. Angry at himself. Feeling guilty, feeling hurt, and—more than anything—feeling confused by it all.

She understood. No, she'd never been to war. No, she hadn't been injured in some horrific event. No, she hadn't spent a lifetime dealing with catastrophic circumstances, but she'd been dealing with men like Aaron for a long enough time. In fact, her father had been one just like him. But the major, as everyone called him, was somebody else now, thankfully.

Having taken over the active business management of this place a long time ago, she'd helped build it to what it was now. The center was her father's pet project, and it had a full team of doctors, physical therapists and counselors. He'd started this massive undertaking, and she'd been more than willing to step in and help carry on. The major was more or less only here for support now … and to help keep spirits up on both sides of the equation.

In the beginning, Hathaway House had been a saving grace for her father. It'd been just the two of them and Gram for so long. Dani's mother had died when she was just a little girl, and she had been raised by her father and her grandmother. Then they had lost Gram too.

She worked here to do everything she could to help these men turn their lives around. The center's work was a gift that kept on giving. As these men healed, the families living in turmoil around them also healed. That part she knew all too well.

When her father had come back from the war, he'd been angry-quiet at times, then explosive and volatile toward others. Broken in body, he had also fractured something in his spirit. He'd been a good man, but he had been through so much that some of that goodness fell through the cracks of this new persona. It had taken a lot of work, and many years, for him to pull it together and become the man he was today.

She knew that love was the answer, but it was more than

love—or rather more than that marshmallow kind of love that people understood when they thought of the word. Sometimes love meant you had to take the hard line and had to force people to do things they didn't want to do. Not necessarily a role she enjoyed, but she had to do it, so she did. And, from the looks of things, Aaron would need a little bit more of the tough love than most of the men who came here.

George would get him settled into his new room. Dani glanced down the empty hallway. Soon she'd go in and officially welcome him, make sure he didn't need anything, and then she'd turn him over to the team who would rally behind him.

Except there were a few secrets in Aaron's case. His medical files should have come with the folder she'd received. She searched her email, and, sure enough, they had been sent along with his other records. Her desk was piled high, so it had to be here somewhere. She spied the large envelope leaning up against the edge of the desk. She pulled back the flap to ensure the file was complete, with X-rays and notes, and … yes, it was. Perfect.

Dani grabbed her clipboard and clamped in a New Resident's Questionnaire, then slipped a couple pens into her pocket and walked down the corridor toward Aaron's new room. He'd been given a spot on the left, facing the horses. All the rooms in Hathaway House were lovely, but, of course, a few were better than others. He had been given one of the nicer rooms as a special request from the donor paying for his stay.

That someone had paid for him was a key issue here. It was expensive to treat the men and women properly. She wished she could open the doors to everybody in need, but the reality was she had not been able to find any state or governmental grant money, so private funding had to cover the bulk of Aaron's costs and fees. Of course insurance covered a lot, but often there was a shortfall. The center ran at a slight loss most times. It took a lot of money to get the specialists and therapists they needed here and to build the equipment prototypes. Only the best would do for these people.

At the doorway to Aaron's room she knocked. She wanted to make sure George was done and Aaron was settled in. When no answer came, she knocked again. When she heard a disgruntled sound inside, she slowly opened the door and peered around the edge. He was lying on his back on top of the bed.

"Good morning."

Aaron rolled to the side and stared at her. He gave a disinterested shrug but said quietly, "Morning."

She walked in with a bright smile and handed him the clipboard and a pen. "I need you to fill out this New Resident form. It shouldn't take too long, and once the paperwork is done, I will let the team know you're ready to see them."

He brought his brows together and stared at her. "What kind of team?"

She knew it wouldn't be the kind he wanted. He would never again be part of the elite military teams who took on some of the most dangerous assignments in the world. Even if they could put him back together again, the military wouldn't take him back. Just the facts of life.

In a gentle voice, she said, "Your medical team." She walked over and hit the buttons on the bed to raise him higher so he could write.

"Oh." His shoulders shook slightly, but he picked up the pen and looked at the paperwork. He went to the first page. She waited—she'd learned long ago that the best way to get the paperwork completed was to not give anybody the option of avoiding doing it.

When he was done, he reached out, returning the clipboard to her. She motioned toward it. "Turn it over. There's a second page."

"Of course there is." With a frown, he slowly made his way through the second set of questions. At the end, he signed his name and held it out again. She took the clipboard, noticing he didn't offer the pen.

"Do you want a notebook and a pen to keep here?"

He shook his head. "A couple should have arrived with my bags."

"Good," she said cheerfully. "But, if you happen to need more, let me know, and I can grab one for you." As she headed toward the door, she said, "Lunch will be in two hours, but coffee is being served in the communal room that George showed you earlier. The wheelchair is yours to use while you're here, or crutches are in the closet, if you'd prefer." At the doorway, she turned to look at him. She motioned with her arm. "Take a left from here for the communal room. Feel free to explore, but please do not leave the main floor. As soon as I get all the paperwork together, I will let the team know you're ready."

Then she left him to his own space and his grim dark thoughts. He had no idea how lucky he was. Hathaway House operated at full capacity at all times with a long waiting list ahead. The donation hadn't been an outright secret, but a note said that the donor preferred to keep his identity under wraps for the moment. She'd do her best to keep it that way.

The same donor had helped several other people, but dozens more were in need. The center did do some pro bono work, but they still had to pay the bills, so only four patients were cared for free of charge and in rotation. As soon as one healed and went home, they went through their files and invited the next candidate to join them. So far the system had worked well.

The last thing she wanted was for Aaron to feel like he was accepting charity. According to his file, his pride was only second in size to his stubbornness. He was a warrior, but warriors also made the worst patients.

Hopefully she was up for the challenge.

Chapter 2

A SHORT WHILE later, Dani returned to Aaron's room. "The paperwork's out of the way." She flashed her brightest, most cheerful smile. "How do you feel now?"

Aaron gave her a shuttered look but answered politely, "I'm fine. Just a little tired after the trip."

She nodded in understanding. "Traveling is stressful. The position you have to sit in often strains your type of injury. Still, you're here now, and once you've had a chance to rest, we can get started on your medical treatment."

Dani pulled up a chair and sat down beside him. "I have a list of your medical team, each of whom you'll meet this afternoon. Everybody will make a point of stopping by to talk to you about the treatments and evaluations that might need to be done." She handed him the sheet from her clipboard. "In preparation for your arrival, the team met to discuss your case."

He took the sheet without a word.

"This is the team who's been pulled together for you—specialists who know and understand what you are going through. You see the name at the top of the first page? Dr. Herzog will be acting as your MD. Below that is your physical therapist, Shane. He's great," she added warmly.

"We have assigned Dr. Klein for counseling." She studied his face for a reaction but still found nothing. "When they arrive, each will go over the treatment you will receive and who else you might need as part of your team. We are team-based here, so, when it comes to getting your prosthesis built and adapted, it'll be all within the same team. We have an engineer on staff who will handle that work."

She glanced at the sheet in his hand again, noting the fine tremor in the paper. "However, everyone needs to work together to get you through the different stages, so you'll have the health and strength and coordination to get used to the prosthesis." Dani looked up and glanced his way to see if he understood.

Only he wasn't looking at her. He studied the sheet of paper she'd given him. "Understand?" she queried gently.

He nodded. "Nothing to understand yet. Except why do I need a counselor?"

She smiled at him. "That's a mandatory part of the treatment. You'll find it fairly noninvasive, and Dr. Klein's a great guy. It's important that we heal not just your physical body but also your emotional body."

"What about my spiritual body? I don't suppose you have an altar here to pray to?" he snapped, sarcasm dripping from his voice.

"No, there's no chapel. However, if you wish something brought into your room or want to speak to a clergy member, we can certainly see to that. We're nondenominational, but we accept all." She smiled at him again and said, "Even you."

He narrowed his gaze at her, as if not sure how to take her teasing.

She laughed and stood, waving her arm around the room in a sweeping motion. She said, "This is your room for the duration of your stay. Most people are here for anywhere from two to ten months, longer if needed. Obviously we do our best to get you self-sufficient fast, so you can continue living the life you want at your own chosen location. However, it's not always possible to get people moving about as much as they would like to be.

"You have your own private bath," she continued, indicating the closed door on the opposite wall. "Some of your work will be done in here. Otherwise, you will be expected to show up at therapy rooms on time and under your own power. If you're not ambulatory enough to do that at any time, then we'll arrange for somebody to come get you. You will need to discuss that with your doctor and your therapist." She spun around to look at him. "You're welcome to dress in your own clothes. However, the therapist will give you a set of comfortable clothes to wear for the physiotherapy sessions to avoid any strain or limits on your ability to do the work.

"Laundry is done once a week. Three meals are provided, at approximately six to nine, eleven to one and dinner runs from five to seven, all in the common area, as well as snacks anytime throughout the day if you're hungry. The schedule is on one of the sheets. We'll start with the basics and move on from there. If the doctor has any dietary requirements for you, or if you have any special food allergies or requests, then tell the doctor," she said. "We have dieticians on staff as well, if you have any concerns."

She continued to run through her spiel, covering all the high points, but she could see his eyes glazing over. She brought her speech to a quick close and walked toward the door. "And remember, this is not prison. However, you are required to stay on the premises all the time. We have day trips into town, and you are always welcome to visit the horses or see the other animals and to wander the gardens whenever you like. Do, please show up for your appointments as required. If you need to go into town, then make the arrangements with me or one of the other staff. We have buses going in on a regular basis." She reached the door. "If you're not up to the day trips and have special requests, staff does shop for residents as well."

"How do I get a hold of you?" His voice was deep, serious, and dark.

"Good question. I'm glad you asked, because I forgot." Upping the wattage of her smile, she fished the cell phone from her pocket and handed it to him. "Everybody at the center gets a basic preprogrammed cell phone to contact every one of your team. My number is right there. We haven't had to take away any phones yet, so please don't abuse it and become the first person where we have to do so."

His lips twitched.

Good. Aaron needed to lighten up. Anything that helped him to feel better was good with her. "Other than that," she said, "I will be around. As I run the center, I'm often at the front desk or in my office. Otherwise, you can find me out with the horses," she added cheerfully. "Over 100 patients are here, and, together with all the support staff, you'll have plenty of people to talk to. It's important that you get out and spend time with others. Everyone is quite friendly, and most are in similar situations to yours."

"And if I don't want to?" He turned and moved his head to look at her. Again, a flat stare.

Her smile hardened just a fraction. "It is your choice of course, but if nothing else, there are beautiful gardens to see and animals who could use a bit of attention. The vet clinic is on the ground floor, and the animals there definitely need to know we aren't here to hurt them."

His gaze narrowed thoughtfully. "You do animal surgeries here?"

"Some. We have a full medical facility for animals and people." She was proud of all they did here. "The local hospital is also an important part of our treatment programs, and the two surgeons who work with us work out of there."

At that, his eyebrows popped up, making her laugh.

"We're a very unusual center, and trying to categorize us will fail."

He gave a clipped nod. "Good. The traditional centers haven't worked out so well for me."

"So give us a chance," she suggested. "You might be pleasantly surprised."

Her phone rang as she stood there. She glanced down at the number and smiled. "That's my call to visit with Helga."

Silence. Then, as she had hoped, he asked, "Helga?"

She raised her smiling gaze to him. "Yes, she's a Newfoundland dog that was hit by a truck. She's getting fitted for a new leg. She's had muscle transplants, and she's doing well. The engineers built a limb that would work, and the vets built a stump that could work with it. She had a few other injuries, but she's a real sweetheart," Dani said warmly. "You'd like her."

"Where is she?"

"Downstairs."

More silence. He contemplated the wheelchair in front of them and then turned to stare out the window. "Maybe another time."

"No problem." She did her best not to show the tiny pang of disappointment she felt inside. It would take time for him to adapt, but she found the animals were the biggest icebreakers of all. People often related to their losses in a way that allowed them to disconnect from their own pain and troubles. They would root for an animal where they'd often given up on themselves.

"Helga will be downstairs for several more days," she said. "After that, we might bring her up to visit."

"Does she have a home?"

Dani shook her head. "Nobody who would claim her. That often happens when an animal is severely injured. Nobody wants to be responsible for the vet's bills."

He nodded. "That might get expensive for you."

She shrugged. "We try not to be too selective. An animal in need is an animal in need." On those words she turned and walked out of the room.

SHE DIDN'T REMEMBER him. Aaron didn't know what to think about that. Except both disappointed and relieved. He wouldn't have to answer difficult questions but then neither did he get a chance to reconnect.

He looked down at the list of team members and, despite his doubts, was impressed that the facility was this organized. He didn't recognize anybody on this list, but at least he had the names to start with. He would research to see if these guys were any good or not. He hoped so, but he didn't expect a miracle anymore. So far the only attempts to get him upright again had been via crutches. While that had worked for a while, his armpits had eventually swollen up badly because they were taking too much of his weight with his bad back. He needed a prosthesis that would work. And he needed his back fixed.

Normally he'd be sent home, entailing multiple trips back and forth for prosthetic limb fittings, but somehow it wasn't working. His stump refused to heal. His back injury, his mental state—he didn't know what else—was hindering his expected progress. So he'd ended up here. Who the hell knew this place even existed?

He certainly hadn't, not before it was brought up as an option. Thank God for his VA benefits because his savings surely wouldn't cover all this. Seemed only fair since he had lost a leg for his country.

He didn't know if the problem was his leg or his back. There'd been talk of more surgery because the stump was so raw. Also talk about surgery on his back. He didn't know if the doctors here were specialists or even if they were likely to be any better than those he'd already seen. All that just because he'd wanted a change of scenery ... That didn't mean he'd needed to transfer here.

Surely Walter Reed should've been enough. Or had someone else had a hand in this move?

Of course he was no longer in the military. Hadn't been for the last six months. Somehow that also meant he was no longer fit for any other job in the military either. SEALs didn't retire and neither did they take on desk jobs in the navy. They weren't geared for it. After being the best of the best, finding out you were now like all the rest was—or worse—disheartening.

He'd heard of many moving on quite happily, and indeed, some of them excelled in their second careers. From another place and time his brother, Levi and Ice, his partner, had set up a new company; and they were hiring ex-military, even if disabled. Maybe down the road ... when he could handle a job. Sure, he was on disability now, but that wasn't the same thing as getting mobile again. Still, he had little to no relationship with his brother. So begging for work was hardly the way he wanted to open the door again.

He wanted off disability as soon as humanly possible. He didn't like charity—from anyone.

So who had helped bring him here—and why?

And what cruel joke did fate play that put Dani in his sights again—the one woman he'd always wanted and couldn't have. Even if he wasn't a SEAL anymore, the honor code among military brothers never ended. Best friends' little sisters—or even brothers' former girlfriends—were always off-limits.

Always.

Yet here she was, taunting him. And, at this stage of his life, he couldn't do anything about it.

Chapter 3

HATHAWAY HOUSE WAS always busy. Today was more so than most. Dani barely had a chance to even consider Aaron's progress weeks in. He was always in the back of her mind. Something was just so sad and defeated about him. She'd read his chart, and she understood the doctors' confusion. Something had stopped him from healing. They figured it was mental and suggested he go to the psychologist. He'd refused. A part of her didn't blame him, but also another part argued, if you continue to do the same thing over and over again, you get the same results. And so far that hadn't worked out for Aaron.

If he wanted to heal he'd have to open up to what was bothering him.

Her father had gone through the same process, when his healing progress had come to a complete halt. Even wanting—or hoping—for improvement was different than this. Like a delicately balanced point in Aaron's medical treatment, and in his life, he could either rush forward and beat it, or he would slide backward in a descent difficult to stop.

She remembered sitting on her father's bed, crying for him to fight, when he'd reached out a hand and asked, "Why?"

It'd stunned her then, hurt her terribly, but she'd come to understand that moment when he gave up. Thankfully her father had turned his mental state around and was now living a completely different life. However, at the time, she'd felt so betrayed. Because, in her mind, she hadn't been enough for him to care about or to fight for, even though in her heart she knew it wasn't true.

She understood that anybody, in the same condition her father had been in, couldn't or didn't want to care about anybody else. They were so focused on how lousy they felt physically, plus how sad and depressed they were emotionally about their supposed nonexistent future, that it was almost impossible for them to relate to how any other person felt. Then, once on that negative pathway, they believed they were a burden to everyone around them and everyone would be better off if they were dead.

Added to that was a lot of them believed everybody else would be better off with them dead. She'd heard more than a few patients at the center bring that up. Depression was a fine-edged sword. It clicked like a light switch, flipping on and off so fast sometimes. That was also why they worked in teams here. If anybody had an inkling that something was going wrong with a patient, they could talk to the rest of the team.

She answered the main landline phone once again while checking her watch. Melissa, her new front office girl, should be coming in any time.

It couldn't happen fast enough. Dani hadn't been in her own office for most of the day because she'd been busy dealing with the front desk and a lot of the other admin responsibilities. Jessica had shown up and then had left early with a family emergency. Of course Dani had stepped in, which meant her work was pushed back again. She had a lot of charts and files to organize, and a never-ending stream of bills to pay. Just as Melissa walked in the door, Dani's other phone rang. She glanced down to see who was calling and smiled. "Hey," she said, delighted to hear the voice on the other end. Levi had been her best friend growing up, and the bond was still strong today.

"How is he?"

"Confused and disturbed. Not understanding how or why he's here. Not depressed but not overjoyed."

"Words like *apathetic, depressed* and *giving up* were what the doctors talked about when I spoke with them," Levi said. "He's my brother, whether he wants to acknowledge the relationship or not."

"We'll do what we can for him," she promised. "At least he's here. That's the hardest part of the battle. And we won't let him out of here until he's strong enough to handle life on his own."

"Good, glad to hear that. Keep my name out of everything, will you?"

"Of course. That shouldn't be a problem as he doesn't remember me. By the way, how is the new company going?"

"So far, so good. I'll do my best not to create any more patients for you."

She laughed at that, then hung up the phone. With a wave and a smile at Tammy, one of the front counter receptionists, she headed back to her office. Levi was a good guy, and he'd helped out with a lot of other cases here. She didn't know what the problem was between him and Aaron, but Levi talked about Aaron, and from what she understood, Aaron did not talk about Levi.

They'd both been injured in military operations. Both SEALs but in completely different locations.

Family was important at times like this. That she well

knew. But if Aaron wasn't willing to open up and let Levi into his life, she could do little to help.

She stopped at her office doorway and shuddered. Her desk was stacked high. George came down the hall toward her, pushing an empty wheelchair back to the front desk. He took one look at her face and said, "You work too hard. Time to shut down and go home for the night."

She waved at her desk overflowing with piles of documents and said, "Really?" She was torn. Part of her wanted to dive in and clear off that pile, and the other part of her wanted to walk away.

George reached over, grabbing the doorknob and pulled the door closed in front of her. "See? Just like that." He gently put an arm around her shoulder and turned her toward the front desk. "You were here at 6:00 a.m., and now it's five o'clock, and you're still here. Go get a meal. Take a break. If you feel like you have to come back, then do so, but you need to rest sometime, Dani."

The trouble was, she knew he was right.

"I hoped to go see Helga again," she murmured as she walked to the front door, wrapping her arms around her chest. Once he'd made the suggestion, exhaustion hit her. "She needed support today."

George laughed. "That dog has barely had one second alone. She's probably wishing all these humans would give her some peace and quiet. We've all been down there multiple times today—you included. Now leave. Go take care of yourself for once."

With a grateful smile, she walked out the front door and stood on the porch, taking several deep breaths. She closed her eyes and let the sunshine and the cool breeze wash over her. A sound from the right made her smile. "Hello, Midnight," she called out.

The answering neigh made her heart light, and her shoulders straightened. No matter how much work was needed to run this place, it was all worth it. Her own home was just on the other side of the tree line—still on the property but separate. She spent every day at the center as it was, so it was important for her to have a bit of space to call her own.

She walked down the steps and over to the fence. Midnight immediately raced toward her. He shoved his big long nose into her hair and neck and blew gently. She stroked the soft felt muzzle and kissed his nose, murmuring sweet nothings to the old horse she'd had since she was just a little girl. She'd done her damnedest to make sure he had a home till the end of his days. He was one of the few fully able-bodied horses on the place. He was hers, and he always had been. Sticking close to the fence, she walked up the line, talking to Midnight as he walked beside her. "It's been a long time since we went riding, hasn't it, buddy?"

He nickered sorrowfully at her side.

At the point where the path turned and headed toward her house, she gave him one last gentle pet and then walked to the house.

"Dad, you home?"

Silence. The inside of the house felt cool, as though nobody had been home all day. Chances were, he hadn't been home at all. He was worse than she was. He'd eat anywhere anytime but only if put in front of him. He no longer cared about meals—he just cared about people and animals.

There were worse things in life. She opened the fridge, spotting the container of leftover stew from several days ago. She brought out a pot and warmed it up. If nothing else, she would eat a hot meal at home tonight. It was beautiful outside, but the last few days had been very stressful. The work was just too much. She needed to hire an extra person but wasn't sure they could afford that.

She reached for her cell phone and called her father. When he answered, she said, "There's a hot bowl of stew here, if you're ready to eat."

He mumbled something about staying and playing cards with somebody downstairs, and he'd eat later. Typical. She dished up some for herself and then went to the table and sat down. The food was delicious, and she was ravenous, but she still couldn't relax. Aaron kept invading her mind. She'd seen a lot of patients come and go at the center. Some stayed a long time, some quickly dealt with what they needed to.

They'd only ever had two cases where they couldn't help. One had ended up with cancer that had metastasized so quickly there'd been nothing they, or anybody, could do for him. The other had refused all help. Dani was bound by the law, and if the patient refused to receive care, Dani could do nothing.

It had broken her heart, but her hands were tied, and she couldn't change the situation. They'd brought in extra specialists and his family members, but nobody could dent the barricade he had around his soul. He'd asked to be shipped home, and that's what they'd done. He'd taken his own life less than three months later.

She hated to think of Aaron heading in either of those directions, but his was a case that defied logic. Sometimes the soul just needed more than what anybody could do for the physical body. Regardless, she was determined Aaron wouldn't become another statistic. Besides, she owed Levi that much. He was counting on her to turn the tide for his brother's sake.

After she finished eating, she stood and washed her bowl. She wished she had brought Aaron's file home with her. It often helped her deal with the residents if she went through their medical histories carefully enough to understand who they were and what made them tick. Sometimes it made for very disturbing bedtime reading, given the injuries that many of them had sustained.

She considered returning to her office and dealing with all that paperwork and then reconsidered. She was just too tired. On the other hand, going to the veterinary section and spending some time with the animals could well brighten her soul instead. Making a quick decision, she grabbed her sweater and almost ran down the hill. Several people were in the common area, and George had been right. Helga was having a hell of a time in the middle of the room. Everybody had a hand or a toy or something for her.

When Helga saw Dani, she barked. Dani walked over, bent down and gave her a big hug. As always, the animals helped restore her good humor. That great big face didn't hurt either. Laughing, she backed away and walked to the other cages where she systematically spent a few minutes with every animal. It was so important for everybody to know somebody cared.

It was the least she could do. So many people had said she couldn't combine humans and animals in the same center, but in her mind, they were a natural pairing. People healed better when they had animals around, and animals healed better when they had people around. To her, that was what a marriage should be all about—a natural pairing. When she finished her tour of the room and was in front of Helga again, she bent down to scratch the big dog and then turned and walked out.

Maybe she would go grab Aaron's file. Take it home with her. She walked upstairs and down the hall, suddenly aware that she would pass Aaron's bedroom. Of course she needed to check in, make sure he was okay. He was the brother of her friend. He had been an old friend of hers too. She wouldn't ignore him.

If her heart whispered that she was caring a little too much, she was well-known for that. She put her heart and soul into this place, and that also meant into every person who walked through the door. His door was open, which she was glad to see, but he was alone, lying in his bed in the dark. She checked her watch. Only seven forty-five. She gave a short knock on the open door, but he didn't move.

"Aaron, it's Dani."

He shuffled and rolled to his back.

She took a hesitant step forward, always aware of people's privacy. "How are you doing?"

"I'm fine."

His voice was riddled with pain. She walked over to the bed. "Did you see the doctors today?"

He nodded. "Yes. And, yes, I had food. And, yes, everybody's been to see me. And, yes, I'm okay."

"Yet you're not," she said bluntly. "I can hear the pain in your voice. I can see it in your body language. Do you need a doctor to see you?"

"No." His voice was cold, hard, with no give in it. She'd seen this before, time and time again. She perched herself on the edge of his bed without asking. Then she reached over and picked up his hand, feeling the scars on his fingers. She didn't remember seeing anything about scar tissue on his fingertips. She'd have to talk to the doctor about it. Maybe they could do something to better heal his fingers.

"Pain comes and goes," she said. "Whether you like drugs or not, there's no healing if you're so twisted up with pain that your body can't function and take care of its own needs."

Even in the shadows of the night, she could see the stiffness of his body, as if he were willing the pain away. She gently stroked his fingers, his palm and the back of his hand. "Even a little bit of pain relief helps the muscles to relax. You've been in a lot of different positions today, and your body wasn't accustomed to all that movement. A muscle relaxant is not a painkiller, but it will have a huge effect on the tension riddling your body right now."

He didn't say anything, and she watched his face until he finally gave a short nod. She patted his hand and stood. "I'll be right back."

Dani went down to the medical room, pulled out her keys and let herself in. She walked to the far wall, where they kept the medications, and she dumped two muscle relaxants into a small cup for Aaron. She walked back to his room, refilled his water flask and then helped him take the two pills. She'd have to remember to add the medication to his file chart and see that he was offered more through the night.

"Thank you," he said, his voice easier.

"No problem. You have a Call button here if you ever need it. You know that, right?"

He nodded.

Of course he knew that, but it would take a hell of a lot more for him to let go of that hard shell of his and ask for help. She walked toward the bedroom door, then said, "Remember, we can all be strong sometimes, but we can't all be strong all the time. I'm glad you accepted this little bit of help because it'll make your healing that much faster."

At the doorway, she paused to say, "Have a good evening."

"How's the dog?"

She dismissed the interruption and stepped back into the room, a warm smile on her face. She kept her tone light and bubbly. "Helga is just lovely. She's getting thoroughly spoiled downstairs."

"Good, and so she should. Every dog should have somebody to love them."

"The same goes for every human being."

"Maybe not those who don't deserve it."

"I don't believe that. Just because you might not think someone deserves it doesn't mean that's true. So often people come here, and they hate themselves for something they either have or haven't done. Or that they're alive, and all their friends are dead. This isn't a case of being deserving. It's a case of you're here, and you need to grow, and you need to heal. If there's anything we can do to help you make that happen, then we'll do it."

He turned his head to face her. "Anything?"

She nodded, a little hesitant, because she'd heard a lot of sexual innuendos in her time, but, willing to give it a shot and see what he was asking, she said, "Within reason of course."

He struggled, grunting, as if asking would be hard.

"What is it you think we can help with?" she asked gently.

"Any chance I can see the dog?"

Her smile bloomed. "Absolutely. How about now?" He stared at her for a moment, his gaze on the wheelchair. He bit down hard on his jaw, but he nodded. He sat up slowly, as if his body would still cry in pain from the day's travels, but then he seemed to relax, as if it wasn't as bad as he'd expected. She brought the wheelchair to him and said, "Do you know how to get into this on your own?"

He looked at her and said, "I think so."

"Well, give it a try."

She stayed at his side, just in case, but knew, if he could succeed at this, it would give him some self-confidence and would help him save face, which mattered to him. His upper torso was strong, even if his back was still showing some damage. His injury limited his range of movement as he struggled into the wheelchair on his own. When he did, he turned to her, his face flushed with success.

"Excellent," she said. "Now let's head in this direction."

She led the way, not offering to push him, but knowing it would be a fine line between him doing this on his own and overdoing it, considering he had had to take a muscle relaxant. When the double doors to the elevator opened wide, they waited for several people to get off, and then she stepped in first, letting him maneuver his way in afterward. She hit the button for the vet clinic downstairs and studied him. He looked better already. Still something was so wrong about seeing reasonably healthy adult males confined to bed. They always looked so much more vibrant when they were up and moving around. She knew, for herself, that it felt that way too.

HELGA *WAS* SPECIAL. He was glad he'd made the effort to see her. The relationship between a man and a dog was something unique. Especially when they were both in need.

However, he didn't want to be in this position. This dog could break his heart. He should leave well enough alone and ignore her. In fact, maybe he shouldn't have come here in the first place. He'd been showing off.

Dani still didn't recognize him. It bothered him, and at the same time, it pissed him off. Sure, it had taken him a few hours but then *bam*. He knew her, but she didn't know him.

How the hell had that happened? To someone like him? Here he was, an invalid, and here she was, running a center, and a massive center at that. Their lives had crossed and changed and parted, apparently to be forgotten forever. He would never have thought such a thing was possible. Back then she consumed his thoughts all the time. The high school, hormonal, teenage-rage years. Tough days. He also had a love-hate relationship with his brother. In truth, he hadn't thought about her since those high school days. Not really. Not often. Not like an obsession or anything. Back then she'd always been Levi's friend. Not one who Levi went to bed with. *Supposedly* ... No, those were his party girls. Back then, Dani had been in a category all her own—his special friend. Somebody who Levi had always confided in and talked with for hours over coffee. He was always at the end of the phone if she called. He'd go running whenever she needed him.

It had never mattered that Aaron had always been in the wings, watching and hurting, because he was not welcome to join in that *special* relationship. In fact, he'd have done anything back then to take his brother's place. Who knew how time would switch their positions and put them in this spot? True, he hadn't recognized her at the beginning. That was most likely from being inundated by so much else. Then, as he'd been lying here this morning, it hit him. It was *her.*

Fate was a bitch. He was finally in a place where she might see him separate from his brother, but he wasn't whole anymore. He'd cut out everything in his life that had to do with Levi, and in a way, she was a big part of that too. Except that, by the time Aaron had cut Levi out of his life, Levi hadn't had anything to do with her for years either. He'd moved on.

At least Aaron thought Levi had. Aaron had a sense of doors opening since coming to her center. How that could be, he wasn't sure. If Levi was opening doors to her, was Levi also opening doors to his brother? To the things Aaron had walked away from?

Aaron wasn't sure he was ready for that. Besides, he hadn't asked to come here. Sure, he'd signed papers to authorize the move. It wasn't like he'd been kidnapped, but ... he'd had no idea *she* was here. He hadn't known what this place was. How could he? He left all that up to his insurance and his VA benefits. That just brought him back to why the hell he was here. How had someone known to put his name on the list? Because Aaron had heard about the long waiting list from the medical team. Maybe he'd been bumped up the line because of someone. He'd be pissed if that was because of Levi and all the people he knew. That was the one connection between Levi, Aaron and Dani aka the Hathaway House. Or it would be the one connection between the three of them, except that she didn't seem to know who the hell Aaron was.

Why the hell was it that the one woman in the world he'd always been interested in would now see him as he truly was—broken?

Chapter 4

DOWNSTAIRS WAS ONLY a shade less noisy than it had been a few minutes ago. The upstairs was wheelchair-friendly, but the downstairs was slightly less so. She opened several doors and waited for him to pass through, making a mental note that they must get powered openers put on these core doors. Once they reached the common room, she could see still a good dozen people sitting with Helga. Dani stood beside Aaron in his wheelchair and said, "Helga, somebody else is here to see you." The Newfoundland lolled on her back, twisting to look at her. She gave a small snuffling bark, seeming to say, "Good. You come here then."

Dani laughed. She'd seen the same behavior in animals and humans alike. They could do whatever the hell they wanted to when nobody was looking, but the minute somebody was there, it was all about getting more attention. She crouched down and clapped her hands lightly. "Come on, Helga. Not everybody has to come to you. You need to get up and work that leg a little bit."

Helga woofed quietly, her big bushy tail wagging in a full sweep across the floor. But Dani refused to move. Instead she sat cross-legged on the cement floor and called Helga again. Then, in a surprise move, Aaron snapped his fingers beside her and said, "Helga, come."

Helga looked over at him and gave a deep woof. She got

slowly to her feet. She was quite able to walk, but now, without the prosthetic leg on, her gait was rather awkward as she made her way to him.

"Nice touch," Dani murmured to Aaron. "Why did you think that would work?"

"Big dogs are usually well-trained. They have to be, otherwise they'd hurt somebody," he said. "But often, when the animal gets injured like that ..." He shrugged. "They get lazy."

Exactly the same for people, Dani thought to herself. But, by then, Helga had already laid her great big head in Aaron's lap, accepting his strokes of attention.

Dani let the two of them enjoy meeting each other, and before long, it was a full-blown cuddle session. Helga crawled into the wheelchair alongside Aaron. He laughed as Helga's big head snuggled up against his face. In another move that half-surprised Dani—she'd seen so many miracles between animals and humans before—she watched as Aaron wrapped his arms around Helga's great big chest and hugged her tight.

Helga didn't mind in the least. She didn't make any move to get away, and indeed, she looked like she was just cuddling closer. She was a big weight to support though. Dani gave them a few minutes, and then she worried it would be too much for Aaron, and he wouldn't know when to stop. She stood and went to grab Helga's collar to pull her back, but Aaron said, "Don't."

At the choked emotion in Aaron's voice, she let her hand drop. If he needed a few minutes longer, then she would give him a few minutes longer. She let her gaze drift to the others in the room, but nobody was interested in what was happening with Helga. In fact, several card games were going on at the far side of the room. She laughed. So this was where her father was. Judging by the stack of busted toothpicks used as betting chips in front of him, he was taking his friends to the cleaners again. "Hey, Dad, how you doing?"

He glanced over at her and smiled. "Doing well. King of the toothpicks."

Her grin widened as the others grumbled. She wasn't sure if they were having a friendly game or if somebody was cheating, but with the particular men involved, she wouldn't be at all surprised either way. At one point, they'd deliberately played games where they would cheat to see how far they could go before the others noticed. All in good fun.

She dropped her gaze to the big man and the big dog next to her. Amazing how Helga wasn't even moving. She was tucked right up against Aaron's chest, all settled in. Dani stroked her silky ears. Finally Aaron straightened and released his hold on the large animal. Helga slipped back slightly, at least enough so she could wash his face with a great big lick. With a chuckle, Dani walked over to the sink and grabbed some paper towels. She dampened them and brought them back for him. "Here. This will help clean up some of that slobber."

"It doesn't matter. She's a beautiful dog."

In fact, she was more than a beautiful dog. She'd make an awesome therapy dog. But Dani'd have to think that concept over. A dog like Helga required a lot of space. Here she would certainly have room for Helga, but Dani couldn't keep taking on every injured animal out there. There were months when she couldn't cover the bills as it were. Still, it was something to consider if Helga had the same effect on patients as she just had on Aaron. With a gentle woof, Helga got down and then sprawled to the floor, stretching out at their feet.

"Do you want to stay down here for a bit longer, or do you want to go back upstairs?" she asked Aaron.

He turned the wheelchair around with a last look at Helga and said, "Let's go back upstairs."

As he maneuvered to the doors leading to the elevator, she said, "You're welcome to return and visit anytime. Just be aware that, on certain days, the place can be frenzied, depending on what surgeries are scheduled."

"I'd like to come back down."

"Have you worked with animals before?"

"I wanted to be a veterinarian, before I went into the military."

"Oh, wow." She felt a jolt at that news but couldn't exactly say why. Levi hadn't mentioned it. Then again he might not know. "I think the animals missed out on something then, during all the years you were in the military."

He shrugged. "Only so many things one person can do with his life."

"Only so many things one person can do with his life *at one time*," she corrected. "You have a whole new future ahead of you. You get to choose what to do now."

She hadn't meant the last line to come out sounding a bit too blunt, but running a place like this made it hard for her to not interfere.

Still her words had an effect, and he was silent all the way back to his room. Once inside, he wheeled himself straight to his bed as she stood hesitantly in his doorway. She knew she should ask if he needed help but had a feeling he would be okay. From the stiff look of his back and the blank look on his face, she figured she was in the way now.

"Okay, I'll leave you for the evening then," she said, backing out. "If you have any trouble getting in and out of bed, or need anything else for the rest of the evening, make sure you call somebody, please." She turned and walked out. No response came from him. No goodbye, no thank you, nothing. Just silence.

She shrugged. Well, she'd take every little bit of progress that she got. The rest would take time.

HOW MANY TIMES would people imply that they knew what was good for him, when they obviously didn't?

He'd been through every damned medical test known to man, so why was he still sitting here in the same place three months later? And all for what? To sit here for another three months and have nothing happen? The doctors didn't know why he wasn't progressing.

But he'd seen Helga down there. She'd progressed faster than he had. Why the hell was that? Even though she'd been beaten and hurt and abused, she still allowed herself to trust people. Maybe she'd learned to trust again while she was here. Maybe being here, in this place, had helped her to heal emotionally. And, as a result, had that emotional healing allowed her to heal physically? Or maybe she'd never lost her sense of trust at all.

He'd certainly done a lot of reading on the subject, and he knew that psychological healing didn't just happen on one level. It had to happen on multiple levels for maximum progress. Well, he'd certainly stalled, and he knew a lot of that had to do with his feelings of betrayal and his lack of trust.

He hadn't gotten his injuries in an enemy skirmish. It would have been bad enough if he had, but this was way worse. No, it was an act of betrayal. He was pretty damn sure Cain had done the unthinkable and gone over to the other side. For money. Only Aaron couldn't prove it.

That made it even worse. He'd loved being in the military, loved being a SEAL, loved being part of something bigger, making a difference in the world. To be one of the best. An honorable profession. Honor was supposed to be in this world. Among his unit. Everyone should follow an honor code, but especially those who fought for their country—particularly a SEAL.

Instead his friend—his best friend—Cain, had gone rogue on a mission. He'd been offered a ton of money to turn his back on his friends, and he'd taken it. He'd blown up the camp himself. Two men dead. Two escaped major physical injury. Cain had disappeared, and then there was Aaron—who couldn't help, who just lay there, fighting the grief for his friends as they'd died in front of him. He had rejoiced for his other friends who, although scarred emotionally by what had happened, could live full healthy physical lives. In fact, they remained in the unit, still fighting the good fight.

But not him. He was caught in between. In no-man's land. He couldn't return to the military. At this point, he couldn't see himself living an aggressively physical life in any way. Yet neither was he dead like his other friends. Unless dead inside counted.

Of course no one understood what bothered him so badly. That anger that consumed him. An anger that never went away. He'd killed several people, all enemies, but the betrayal of his best friend still ate at him. How could Cain have done this to his unit? They were all good men. How did one turn his back on people and say, "Screw it?" And blow them all up?

He stared down at his hands as they slowly fisted once again. He worked on his breathing, trying to regulate it before rage overwhelmed him. An anger-management issue, the doctors had called it. A refusal to accept his current circumstances. He'd seen shrinks, but he hadn't opened up. How could he?

No one believed him.

He'd seen Cain's laughing face as he had pushed the remote on the detonator. A detonator that Aaron hadn't realized was in his buddy's hand until it was too late. Even then, he wouldn't have believed it was rigged to blow. Who would? They were at war—but not with each other.

Then it was too late. As the ground around him exploded, he'd realized the truth. Only Cain had disappeared. Forever. As far as the military was concerned, he was classified as missing in action. Aaron had tried to tell the brass what had happened until he was blue in the face. Nobody listened. Maybe they were listening on the sly, but publicly there would never be that acknowledgment. It didn't happen. SEALs didn't go rogue. There was no such thing as a mole inside a SEAL unit.

Aaron didn't give a damn what they called it. He just wanted somebody to say he'd spoken the truth. Then he wanted somebody to hunt down and kill that asshole Cain. David and Mark did not deserve to die. Both damned good men. That Cain could've done that to his SEAL brothers defied logic. It made Aaron look twice at everybody he thought he knew, as if they were all strangers. Maybe many of them were—maybe they were ready to turn around and stab him in the back.

So, although he'd spoken to several shrinks, he hadn't given them all of his festering anger because they were all military too. After he had been branded a liar, it was hard to go backward. Every time they didn't believe him was like being called a liar all over again. That ate at him too. He'd written several letters to the commander, hoping somebody would listen to him, but the responses he'd received were lukewarm, and they just wished him a speedy recovery.

Basically they figured he was just dealing with sour grapes. Maybe he was. But it was more than just his inability to get off this bed and hunt down that asshole who put him here. For David and Mark's sake, and for his own. Stephen and Charlie had moved on with their lives. They'd survived, and Aaron wasn't involved with them anymore. They hadn't seen what had happened—they hadn't seen Cain's face.

In fact, it was worse because they'd figured Aaron had caused the bomb to blow. They said that he'd been careless and that he'd caused an accident by not looking after the equipment properly. That Cain had gotten away with this and that Aaron should be branded as the responsible party was just too much to let go of.

That brought his mind back to Helga. Maybe if he was a dumb dog, then he could forget, but he wasn't. He was a man caught twisting in a web of lies and a grief that ate at him. He leaned back on his bed and slowly breathed out. In a low voice, he muttered, "Goddammit. I will avenge those deaths."

"Will avenging those deaths make you any happier?"

He froze. Damn. He forgot he was almost never alone anymore. Ever since the accident, orderlies, nurses, or doctors were around. Those well-meaning folks who had good intentions for his health. He rolled his head sideways and glared at Dani. "You can leave now," he said pointedly.

She smiled. "Of course I can. So can you." She turned and walked out.

Instantly he felt like a heel. He wasn't angry at her. In fact she was one of the nicest people he'd seen in a long time—and sexy as hell. Of course now he looked like an angry, vengeful asshole. That wasn't what he meant either, but, as he lay here, he'd realized he couldn't let it go. He sat up and wondered about going after her. It was evening. It was late. Surely she didn't live in the center by herself, did she? He glanced down at the phone she'd left beside him, picked it up, and pressed her contact name, not allowing himself to second-guess his actions.

As soon as she answered, he blurted out, "I'm sorry. I didn't mean to take out my anger on you."

Her light laughter warmed his heart. "That's fine, but you do need to work on forgiveness and letting go. I'm sure I'm not the first person to tell you how it hinders your healing."

"No, you aren't." He sighed, still very irate at himself and at the world in general. "The trouble is, just because people say I should forgive, doesn't mean they give any solid instructions about how to make that happen. When you're angry, when you're full of rage, not even at the circumstances but at somebody specifically that you can't even talk to, to clear things up ..." He closed his eyes and rubbed his forehead. "Anyway, I'm sorry." He quickly hung up the phone. He was a fool to call. A fool to even apologize. He was here to deal with his shit. She had to be used to it. He just hadn't wanted to be yet another asshole in her day.

Chapter 5

T HE TWO SIBLINGS, Levi and Aaron, possessed more testosterone than a whole naval ship full of men. Dani had never understood how that was possible. She had no siblings, but her father wasn't full of conflict, although he was a big gruff, strong male presence. He wasn't aggressive or looking for confrontation. So she'd grown up not expecting that. Yet, whenever she'd seen the two brothers together, they'd almost frightened her with their intensity.

Levi had always been quick to reassure her that she was never in any danger. That this went on all the time. Well, that might be, but it wasn't comfortable for her. Now that she saw Aaron in his present shape, she wondered if she should mention something about knowing him. But it had been a long time ago, and she didn't want to bring up any possible connection to Levi. Because he didn't want Aaron to know who was paying for his treatment. She smiled. It was an interesting and heartwarming development in their relationship, but, at the same time, it was complicated. She sighed. There were always complications.

Still, it was nighttime, and a whole new day awaited tomorrow. Back home, she undressed and got ready for bed. She needed a good night's sleep. They'd had the odd break-in over the last few years but nothing major. They had installed a new security system, but she was still getting used to it. Every once in a while the alarms went off and woke her up. A few days ago, the alarm had gone off several times. She woke up to the slightest sounds now, waiting to see what had bothered her.

Hopefully tonight she'd sleep all the way through.

When her alarm woke her at six, Dani yawned and stretched, feeling pleased. A whole night's sleep for herself, where she hadn't woken up once. So a good night at the center too. She checked her phone just in case, but Aaron's was the last call.

It was early enough that she could get out for an hour on her own. She grinned. She would slip out for a horseback ride. She dressed quickly and headed to the stables. She'd take out Sable, a younger mare, who had been with her for years. The horse had been abused and, as a result, was often afraid of men and of being closed in. Her stall was always open to the field behind. That way she could come and go as she wanted.

Dani threw a western saddle on her and cinched it up. Instead of a bit in the horse's mouth, she placed a bosal over her nose and draped the reins across her neck. She led Sable out to the sunshine, where Dani hopped on with the ease of long years of practice. Calling out to Midnight to join them, she led the way to the back fields. They had several hundred acres here, and the ranch backed up to thousands more of open range.

If she did nothing more than ride the fence line, looking for potential problems, it would make her happy. The sun was up, the heat was down, and fresh air blew gently across the fields. It was hard not to think of a more perfect day. With Midnight keeping pace at her side, they followed the fence line. Dani was thankful it was in good shape.

However, she realized it had been a while since she'd had the farrier in to trim hooves. All the animals needed regular maintenance too. A good one was just down the road who often did the work pro bono. An added blessing. She'd have to remember to give him a call when she got back.

Only, by the time she'd finished her ride, her phone rang, and when she finally made it to the center, she discovered that chaos reigned. One patient was set to leave, and his ride hadn't arrived. Another patient was transferring in, and he'd come in several hours early. His room wasn't ready because the other patient hadn't left. She smiled at everyone and did her best to ease the situation. She called for help.

"We'll get this sorted out immediately," she said in her best calm administrator's voice. "In the meantime, let's get everybody settled as best as we can."

She took charge and led the new arrival to the deck and had a fresh cup of coffee brought to him. Her father was handy, so she grabbed him and told him to visit. By the time she'd gotten the room cleaned out, the departing patient was settled on a different part of the deck, waiting until his ride showed up. Another quick sort out done, and the new patient was settled in his room too. With a beaming smile, she walked through the place into her office, closed the door and exhaled loudly. "Oh, thank God."

These mornings when unexpected things happened were challenging, but they were usual occurrences in centers like this. They had over seventy part-time and full-time staff members, and sometimes life just happened. Sometimes in a good way. Sometimes in a bad way.

She sat down at her desk and stared at the flashing light on her telephone. With a sigh, she picked up a pen and notepad, and ran through her voicemail messages. After that, she checked her email and discovered dozens of new messages requiring immediate responses. Rubbing her temple, she realized it would be one of those days.

She got up, poured some coffee and then did a quick walk around to see how Aaron was doing—a better way to start her day than all the pressing emails and phone calls. She stopped at his room. The door was shut, so she gave a quick knock. "Aaron, it's Dani. How are you doing this morning?"

No answer. She frowned. Given the security and privacy rules they had established, along with common courtesy, she could hardly walk in on him. Instead, she continued on. She quickly did the rounds, stopping in and visiting with several people in need of a boost. Impulsively she slipped downstairs and found Helga in the middle of the room in front of her adoring audience, with Aaron on the floor with her. She stopped in the open doorway and smiled. This was better than she could've hoped for. They were fitting Helga with a new cup for her stump, but she wasn't interested. She kept kicking it free. The stump had healed enough on one side, but she'd had an accident and had bruised up the other side pretty good. Dani walked over and reached down to cuddle Helga's head, helping to calm her while the men fitted her new back leg.

"Good timing." Stan, the vet, turned to look at her with a big smile.

She glanced over at Aaron and smiled. He reached up and stroked the big dog across the belly. "She's a beautiful dog."

Stan laughed. "She's got the best personality, but she's awfully big to push around when she doesn't want to do something."

"So we make sure the right thing to do is easy, and the

wrong thing is difficult," Dani said with a grin. That was a familiar phrase of her father's, one that an old cowboy had taught him.

"Isn't that the truth?" They finally buckled on the leg, and then they helped Helga onto her feet. They watched as she walked awkwardly around the room, adapting to the new prosthesis. Stan looked over at Dani. "We don't usually see you around here in the morning."

"You shouldn't be seeing me now either," she said with a laugh. "My email inbox is full. My voicemail is overloaded, and my to-do list is out the door." Her grin widened. "Hence I'm hiding."

The two men grinned at her. She loved that smile of Aaron's, with just a hint of likeness to his big brother's. She had never really seen it before. "You look so much like your brother right now." The words slipped out before she could stop them.

His smile fell away, and he stared at her. In a quiet voice, he said, "I didn't think you remembered me."

Her eyebrows shot up, and she scrambled to cover up her slip. "Not remember you? How is that possible?" She forced a wicked grin. "The two of you are very memorable."

She watched the flush of pink staining his neck and smiled.

To give him a moment, she turned her gaze at Stan, who had been watching the exchange with interest. "I knew Aaron when he and his brother were still living together, years ago. We were all a whole lot younger then."

"We were," Stan said. He reached up to pat the salt-and-pepper hair on his head and added, "Still not longing to go back there for anything. I'm quite happy with this stage of life right now."

He returned his attention to Helga and said, "I'll take her out back to one of the runs and see how she does on her own, when we're not all around to give her this much attention."

"Good idea. I'd better make my way upstairs again." She turned to Aaron and added, "Did you come down here in your wheel—?" He was standing, having gotten his crutches under him.

She nodded approvingly. "Crutches are hell on the armpits," she said, "but there's just something nice about being on your feet."

He inclined his head and slowly hobbled past her. She studied his movements, realizing that, even with lots of experience and knowing how to use them correctly, the crutches still pained him.

She followed Aaron to the elevators and stepped inside with him. As the double doors opened onto the main floor, she asked, "Are you interested in having a coffee?"

"Are you asking Levi's younger brother, or are you asking me, as I stand before you now?"

That jolted her into turning and staring at him in surprise. "Well, I have no problems with having coffee with Levi's little brother, because I quite liked him way back then, the same as I liked Levi. However, I would like to have coffee with Aaron, as he stands in front of me now."

Boy, had that opened up a whole different set of attitudes she hadn't expected. Maybe something deeper and darker rooted was involved in their sibling rivalry that she didn't know about. She would have to talk to Levi and get the details. Maybe that's what was holding Aaron back. That little bit of resentment could cause wounds to fester inside and out. He didn't need to completely bare his soul in order to heal, but it did need to be cleaned out.

They walked onto the deck, and she was overjoyed to see the sun still shining. They passed George, and he grinned at them. "You guys going to relax for a little bit?"

She laughed at him. "It does happen. Maybe not enough but it does happen."

"I'm heading to the kitchen. Can I get you some coffee?"

She beamed up at him. "Two coffees would be lovely. Thanks, George."

He waved over at the far side and said, "Go grab a comfy chair. I'll be back in a few minutes."

She collapsed onto one of the deep cushions along the far corner as Aaron sat down at the table beside her. "Today would be a perfect day to play hooky. Except I have so much work to do."

"If you need a day off, then take it," he said. "Life is way too short, as I'm finding out."

"Well, playing hooky when you're all alone isn't much fun. If I had a boyfriend, then maybe. Or a best friend to go for a long bike ride ..." She shrugged. "As it is, I have a ton of work to do. So I should just focus and get that all done."

"How is it that you don't have a boyfriend?" he asked, astonishment written across his face. "I'm sure lots of the guys are falling all over you. You're gorgeous and look at the work you're doing here."

She smirked. "If you remember way back when, guys weren't falling all over me then either. I was falling all over *them*. I had more crushes than any girl my age. But I was also a klutz. I fell every time I tried to wear high heels, and every time I put on makeup, I looked like a clown." She waved at the vast area behind them. "This is finally me. Natural. Jeans and a T-shirt. What you see is what you get."

"Still one thousand guys should be lining up to see what you've got," he said calmly. "I don't remember any of the rest of that, because I had a crush on you so bad back then."

Her laughter fell away, and she leaned forward to stare at him. "Honestly?"

He nodded, and that grin she'd only seen once or twice, but remembered from way back when, peeked out. It was a heart-stopper. With a little bit of a hook on the side, meant to reach out and grab the heart and yank. She felt herself yanked right now. "No way."

"Oh, yes way."

"Why didn't you say something?"

"Because you were my brother's girl. How could I say anything to you?"

She fell back against the seat cushion and stared at him. "I was never Levi's girl. Levi was my best friend. I was one of his best friends, but we were never boyfriend and girl-friend—and definitely not lovers for that matter."

Aaron settled back to stare at her, his gaze intense, as if deciphering whether she told the truth or not.

She opened her arms and held out her hands. "Honest-ly."

He turned his head to stare off into the distance, and she wasn't sure just how this discussion had changed something, but it had. As if something fell off his shoulders, and he could sit easier. Taller.

His revelation affected her too. She wasn't even sure how, but it did. She'd always liked him, but in her head, he was Levi's little brother. Just as off-limits as he apparently felt she was.

Sad. But very interesting, given where they were now.

GEORGE DROPPED OFF their coffees and left them to themselves again.

Aaron stared across the long green and grassy fields ahead of them. His mind churned. She hadn't been Levi's girlfriend? There hadn't been anything between them? He tried to cast his mind back and remember exactly what Levi had said, but too many years had gone by. Too many arguments between them. Too many heated words exchanged in anger to remember anything for sure.

He'd certainly had the impression that not only were they boyfriend and girlfriend but that they were lovers. Had it been Levi who had put that idea into Aaron's head, or had Aaron just assumed that fact, and Levi had let it ride? That would've been Levi too. If Aaron had jumped to a conclusion without asking, Levi would just ignore his brother and let the assumptions go on. He'd always been like that.

What possible reason would there have been for him to lie to Aaron? Unless Levi didn't want Aaron to know that they weren't lovers. Maybe Levi wanted to be closer to Dani back then. It would look like a failure in his eyes if Aaron had assumed that they had that level of a relationship and they hadn't. Aaron almost smiled at the thought. He also hadn't exactly been a prize himself back them. There'd still been a ton of anger, and he had been on the wild side.

If Levi was a good friend of Dani's, he might not have wanted Aaron anywhere around her. Levi always was protective. He'd always been a champion of the underdog, standing up for the little guy. For a long time, Aaron had resented that. As the younger brother, he felt his older brother should have stepped back earlier. Only Levi didn't seem to know how.

Then they were two brothers with a different mother, and that made a difference too. After his own mother had died, he'd gotten wild. Levi had already lost his mother and had a more distant relationship to Aaron's mother. Although cordial, they weren't close. Their father had insisted on good relationships on the surface—for the public to see. Yet, as Aaron thought about it, he realized Levi had been the spitting image of their father—who was an abusive bastard when out of the public eye—not taking after those tendencies though, just carrying on his father's looks. So Levi'd been closer to their father while Aaron had been closer to his mother. He'd bugged Levi about it a lot growing up.

By the time Aaron became an adult, after a tumultuous few years, just enough distance was between the two of them to separate them. After his mother's death when he was fourteen, he'd gone a little crazy. He was angry at life and everyone in it who wasn't hurting the same as he was. That included Levi. As he grew up, he'd made no attempt to cross the growing divide between them. Only three years were between the brothers, but it might as well have been sixteen.

He hadn't even thought about if his brother was distressed by the loss of his second mother. Mostly because he'd been so sure Levi wasn't. Yet how could he not have been? He'd spent fourteen years with her. There had to be some connection.

Of course he'd never asked Levi. She just arrived one day, and for a while, she was there all the time. Of course, if Aaron were Levi, he'd have taken her to bed. The two brothers were both healthy young males, and that had been the drive back then. He stared down at his hands and frowned. Not so much anymore.

"Thoughts?" Dani's gentle voice broke into his trip down memory lane.

He gave a hard shake of his head but managed a gentle smile for her. "Levi and I have been at loggerheads for a long time. I thought something was a given back then but wasn't."

Her smile bloomed. "I never lost track of him," she admitted. "We'd talk every now and then. When he went into the military, he took a different path, and he became so immersed in it I think a lot of us just felt left out."

"Levi is like that. Very focused." Aaron wasn't exactly sure how to feel right now. He'd been seriously crazy over Dani back then. Had he known she wasn't with his brother, would that have changed the outcome years ago? Or what potential lay before them right now? If he had ever hated what he'd become, it was now. He wasn't a whole man. He wasn't sure what he would do for a job or career. It wasn't like he would be the solid provider he'd always expected to be.

"Levi's turned his life around. His injuries were bad, but he's recovering," she said with a smile. "Even better is that he's not in the military, and now he has a whole new company and a whole new life." She spread her hands on the table, and with her gaze directly on Aaron's, she said, "I'm proud of him."

Aaron swallowed hard. He wanted to be proud of his brother. He wanted to think such feelings existed. But he wasn't sure they'd ever get past all the other garbage they'd had growing up. As he looked back, even he could see that a lot of it was caused by his own anger problems. "I haven't talked to him in years," he said. "I'd heard he'd been injured, but by the time I got the whole story, he was back on his feet and doing fine again."

"Well, it certainly wasn't that fast, but he is definitely back on his feet. He's running a private security company here in Texas right now." She picked up her coffee and took a sip. "I don't know what happened between the two of you, but he's certainly hiring a lot of former military men for his company."

"Ex-military doesn't mean damaged and disabled," he said, his voice hard. The last thing he wanted was charity.

"Well, he's got Stone, Merk, and Rhodes with them. They were injured as well in the blast that caught them all up—although not as badly, I believe."

"Right, the men in Levi's unit. Levi's secret unit. The best of the best." That must've been very hard for his brother. "Maybe he started the company so his unit would have employment." He almost laughed at that. It took a hell of a lot of effort and time, not to mention money, to set up a company. Most people wouldn't do that just to give a few friends a paycheck.

"Oh, I don't think so. Maybe it started out as something like that, but he's gotten pretty big. I think a good dozen-plus men work for him now. They are looking at opening a second office on the West Coast too."

Tempting. But he was a long way away from doing something like that. Interesting that Levi took on disabled men. Giving them a new life. Aaron knew a lot of vets who had less than a full life. In fact, they were living on the streets, surviving day-to-day, while trying to find new purpose in their world gone crazy. So many vets just stayed at home and watched TV.

Not the life for a warrior. Even after the war was over.

Again it didn't matter, because he wasn't whole. Yet, he

couldn't keep that thought from rolling around in the back of his mind.

"So back to when you had a crush on me," she said in a teasing voice. "I never knew. I'm surprised."

He snorted. "I'm not. Back then I was a very angry teenager. I'd lost my mom a few years earlier and pretty much hated the world. I wouldn't have let you know anything back then. My father drilled a few things into us both that Levi and I agreed upon. *Integrity and honesty.* A combination of traits that's very hard to come by in this world. But Dad forgot all that when he had a bottle in his hand." He picked up his coffee cup and stared at the thick black brew. "Because somebody else didn't follow those simple rules of ethics is why I'm here."

She leaned forward to stare at him. "What do you mean?"

He wrestled with himself. Should he tell her? Would it just put her off? Come across as sour grapes? On the other hand, she'd read his file and likely some notes were in there about him fielding the blame, accusing a fellow officer.

He settled back, looking for a way to change the conversation.

"No," she snapped at him. "You can't say something like that and then walk away. Obviously this is very important to you. I need you to tell me what's going on."

Woodenly he placed his cup back on the table and brushed away nonexistent crumbs. "You won't believe me," he muttered.

"That's not true. I can't make a decision as to whether I believe you or not if I don't know exactly what your story is."

He glared at her. "The military doesn't believe me, so why would anybody else?"

"I'm not anybody else."

She had said it so simply, he realized the truth. She wasn't coming from a background of protecting the military. She was somebody looking from the perspective of healing.

He took a deep breath and slowly explained about being in Afghanistan and how they'd been expected to face enemy fire and deal with the dangers of landmines on a daily basis. It wasn't that they didn't expect to be injured—they always knew it was a possibility—but because they were doing what was right and protecting their country, they just always shrugged it off.

He stopped talking for a long moment. She reached across and cupped his fist in her hands. His white-knuckled fist. He made himself continue.

"I'm an EOD specialist," he said with a humorless smile. "At the camp, we were sorting through our supplies. We were making explosives for a run to be done the next day. I had four men with me. Two were working off to the side, but two were right beside me. I looked up to see my best friend, Cain, standing there in front of me, with an odd look on his face. Then he said something weird. He said, 'Have a nice life,' and then he turned and walked away. I studied him for a long moment, confused, and then I called out, 'What are you talking about?' He turned and held up a device in his hand. A detonator. He said, 'I'm sorry, but this is what I mean,' and he pushed the button.

"I was already running toward him, hoping to stop him. The blast lifted me up and threw me a good twenty feet away. I woke up in the hospital to find out my two other buddies had taken the blast full-on. The two off to the side survived with just a few scrapes. Of course I lost my leg and damaged my back." He forced his fingers to open wide and spread them across the table as she continued to cover his hands with hers. He stared down at her long slim fingers resting against his big thick muscled ones. He shook his head.

"It wouldn't be so bad if it wasn't such a betrayal." He gave an ugly laugh. "No, it still would be as bad. Because nobody in the military believed me."

She leaned forward. "What do you mean, they didn't believe you?"

"They didn't believe Cain deliberately blew us up."

She sat back, a look of shock and disbelief on her face. "Did Cain die in the blast?"

"Cain is listed as MIA," he said calmly. "But he was running damned fast in the opposite direction of the blast when I was after him. So …" His anger spiked. "Missing in action might be the truth, but if that's the case, he's missing because he wants to be."

"That's horrible," she cried.

He realized he had to get the last of it out. "It's worse than that. Because they didn't acknowledge Cain had done this deliberately, and they needed to look for reasons, they put the blame on me, saying I had been careless. That it was my fault everything blew up. Essentially saying I killed my friends."

Then he sat back, feeling the same damned wall of defeat crushing in on him.

Chapter 6

BACK IN HER office, Dani sat in her chair and stared out the window for a long moment. Betrayal, as root causes go, was a big one for Aaron. She didn't blame him one bit, and she could also see how that betrayal was compounded by those who he had trusted, respected and looked up to. Not believing in him was creating this massive pit of anger. No wonder he wasn't healing. She wasn't sure what she could do to help, but he had to do something to move past it.

The only person she knew with those kinds of connections was Levi, but she wasn't sure he even understood what his brother had been through. It would be a betrayal again, from her, if she were to talk his brother about this without Aaron's permission. If he had wanted Levi to know, then Aaron would've called and told his brother himself. Yet a part of her mind understood that thanks to the estrangement, Aaron wouldn't say anything to Levi.

Her fingers itched to grab the phone and call Levi. But she held back. It was very much a tangled web right now. She had a history with both of them but not enough of a history, according to Aaron. She still couldn't get over the fact that he had had a crush on her. Because she'd had a crush on him back then too. Levi had told her that Aaron was a bad deal. He was messed up and needed to get his head straight before anybody could spend time with him. She had believed Levi because she trusted him. Maybe he had been right back then. When she listened to Aaron talking about the loss of his mom and the anger about his brother, when she remembered the bits and pieces that Levi had said to her, she could see how all that would gel.

The thing was, Aaron was still a bit of a messed-up guy right now. One vague idea of how to help came to her, but she figured he might get very angry about how it came to be. So, if she had any feelings forming, or if she wanted any relationship with him, she would have to kiss all that goodbye because he would never forgive her for crossing the line.

Not that any relationship interested her at the moment. Not after Jim. And a lot of the residents here were either clingy or straightaway asking her to marry them—she'd had something like seventeen proposals over her time at Hathaway House. Then others were standoffish and didn't want anything to do with single women. That usually stemmed from a belief they were no longer whole men. They were incapable of being who they used to be, and therefore, who they were now was less than satisfactory. So, an already attached woman was less threatening to them.

Of course that wasn't true. So often they were much better men now because of what they'd been through. Then again it was also unprofessional to have a relationship with a patient—unethical, if not downright illegal between a doctor and a patient. So, even though she was not a doctor, she'd avoided even the smallest hint from any of the patients like the plague. Which was why Aaron's presence was suddenly very confusing. The rules had always been black-and-white for her, until he arrived and brought his own set of problems with him.

Aaron was also the only patient she'd known in the past, before they came here. Maybe that made the difference.

She picked up the phone once again and immediately put it down. She needed his permission to bring this to somebody else's attention. She ran her hands over her face.

"What do I do?" she whispered to the empty room. "I didn't tell him our conversation would be confidential." But she also knew it would be a betrayal, no matter how she looked at it. As she sat here, wrestling with the dilemma, her phone rang in her hand. She turned to look at the number and froze. As if Levi had read her mind. She answered the call, her voice tentative.

"How is Aaron doing?" Levi asked.

She was stumped. She didn't know what to say.

"What's the matter?" This time Levi's voice had a hard edge. "Has he had a relapse?"

"No," she said slowly. "In fact, maybe it's a break-through, but I don't feel I can discuss it with you because it's confidential. But ..."

"But what?"

"Something's holding him back from healing. I just don't know how to help him get through this."

"Shrink?"

"No. Maybe justice?" She winced. That was the can opener for ten more questions. Questions she didn't have answers to. She brightened. Maybe if Aaron would tell Levi ... "I guess there's no chance you can come in and talk to him, is there?"

"I don't think so. He doesn't want to see me," Levi said calmly. "I haven't seen him in a long time now."

"You might be able to help him with something. Some-thing that your specialized skills and connections could possibly get him answers to." Then she took a big breath and continued. "Maybe not. He says the case is closed, and he's been blamed. There's probably nothing anybody can do."

"Case closed? Blamed? What the hell happened?"

"Shit. I didn't mean to say that blame part, honest," she cried out. "I'm no good at keeping secrets. But ethically I can't say anything. Something is wrong. Something is stopping him from moving forward."

"His accident?"

She didn't answer. How could she?

"I'm on it. I heard about what happened, but I didn't believe it at the time. Still, shit happens to all of us sometimes. Let me look into it." He hung up.

She placed her phone on her desk and stared at it. Then the tremors started. Oh, dear God, what had she done? If Aaron ever found out that she had talked to Levi about this, Aaron wouldn't ever speak to her again. Any potential friendship, let alone a relationship with this man, drifted right out of the window. He'd already been betrayed twice, by Cain, then the navy—a third betrayal would be too much. "I didn't betray you," she whispered into the quiet room. "I didn't mean for it to slip out. But Levi is the best person to resolve this."

She shook her head. It didn't matter. There was no redeeming this. She wasn't one to take half measures, and she'd certainly blown it wide open this time. The only thing she could hope for was that Levi did find something to fix this problem and potentially to provide the avenue for Aaron to move on with his life. Sure, he also had a bit more reconstructive surgery to go through and more therapy to deal with, but he wasn't far from being a fully able male again. However, he had to get his mind focused on his healing, off his revenge on Cain and clearing Aaron's name with the navy.

She studied all the paperwork on her desk needing her attention and realized that, if nothing else, she had a perfect diversion to keep her mind off of what she had just done.

Her trick worked for several days. She stopped in to say hi to Aaron on a regular basis. She was nearly successful in convincing herself the whole thing would wash away, and it wouldn't have any effect on their renewing friendship. Then, at odd times, she'd remember how she'd let the cat out of the bag, and she'd wince and realize just how delicate balancing her relationship with Aaron truly was.

"This is bad news, any way I look at it," she muttered to herself once she was back in her office again.

She loved the long glances between them, the bright smile when he saw her, her uncontrollable urge to see him, her daily detours so she could catch a glimpse of him. Obviously something was developing between them, but it was bittersweet. She just felt like she was in quicksand, and if she said the wrong thing, it would all slip away. Whenever she felt like that, she'd sit down and say, "If I have to sacrifice my relationship with him in order to have him healed, then so be it."

But she wanted both.

She dove back into work to bury the fear and panic of losing him once again. All those years she'd been out of touch, it had been easy to believe he'd moved on with his life and was probably happily married with the prerequisite two-and-a-half kids.

Then the tears rose, and she realized she would lose him forever this time if he found out.

She shook her head and snapped at herself. "Stop being a

fool."

She got another file and opened it, determined to whittle down some of this never-ending paperwork in front of her. When her phone rang, she didn't think about it. She just grabbed it and answered it.

"Dani, I want to see Aaron."

Levi. She sucked in her breath. "Do you think that's a good idea?"

"I think I have to. I've found some information, but I need to confirm the details with him."

"The thing is, I didn't tell him that I told you any-thing—"

"And you didn't tell me anything. Nothing that I hadn't already heard anyway. But I do have some questions. If I am to find a solution to this, I need to talk to him."

"By phone?" she asked hopefully.

"No. I think this is better done in person." An awkward silence followed, where she tried to figure out how bad this would be for her, when he added, "Is something going on between the two of you?"

Maybe? "No," she answered in a shaky voice. "I just feel like I did something wrong by telling you that little bit I did."

"If it's meant to be ..."

"Easy for you to say. I know he already feels like he's been betrayed by everybody. I just can't be one more in the long line of people who he can't trust."

"If you believe this is holding back his healing, then this is what he needs to do to get better. Isn't it worth it for his sake?"

She pinched the bridge of her nose, and even though hot tears burned the corners of her eyes, she nodded. "Absolutely. It's worth it for his sake. I'll just be collateral damage," she said bitterly. "But who cares, right?"

"Don't look at it that way," he said, his voice softening. "My brother's not a fool. It might be a little bit rocky for a while, but he'll understand why you did it."

"Will he?" she said willfully. "Well, I guess it's better now, before we get any farther into what might or might not have been."

"Good. I'm flying in tomorrow morning."

And he hung up. Again.

WHEN AARON WOKE this morning, he was still cussing himself out for having spoken like he had with Dani. It had been days, but it still ate at him. He was a private man and didn't want pity from anyone—especially her. Like he'd gone back in time to be that teenager, so in love with the classy girl in front of him, that he'd been awkward as hell. He hadn't been trying to woo her, but he'd certainly been honest, and she'd listened. He was grateful for that, but he hadn't wanted to dirty what was between them. Of course assuming something *was* between them.

He got up and worked his way to the shower. He hoped the stream of hot water would improve his mood. He had been fiercely independent from the beginning, but some things were just impossible to do. He had his crutches, but that was also damned hard on his back. The doctors had some special surgery they'd wanted to do, but he'd been resisting. Now he was wondering why he was so against it.

He figured he should have a working prosthesis, so that if his back wasn't strong enough, at least he could still walk.

Unfortunately he hadn't improved to the point of getting the prosthetic limb he wanted.

Moving carefully, he headed to the bed where he slowly dried off, then dressed. No way would he wear hospital clothes again. They'd given him one set for all the tests, but he'd been quick to change back into his everyday clothes. The thing was, he didn't have very many of those either, and he wasn't taking the damn Hathaway House bus to buy more, but as soon as he got the damned address of this place, he planned to order some online.

That thought stopped him outright. He let out a short, sharp laugh. Since when had shopping therapy been a solution to his problems? Still, if it would help, then he'd take it. He looked around for his schedule, trying to remember what was on tap this morning.

So far, everybody had treated him fairly delicately, but he knew the kid gloves were coming off on the physio pretty damned soon. Shane was already notorious for hard work and pushing Aaron past the point of exhaustion. Yesterday had been more about seeing how far he could work and how much strength he could apply. He figured today he would get his ass kicked. The one good thing about this place was that, after they'd done their tests, they'd quickly brought in support bars that helped him get in and out of bed. In fact, just enough extras were attached to his bed that he could do a lot more for himself. He realized that having independence went a long way to improving his mood as well.

Of course these extra mobility aids could very quickly become torture instruments too. He didn't doubt it. Some of the bars had pulleys and weights attached to the sides, so who knew?

He sat on the bed, beads of sweat still rising on his forehead, even after he was finally dressed. He wondered if he should use his crutches or the wheelchair to get to the breakfast buffet. He checked his watch. He was running a bit late, but using the wheelchair seemed like giving in. If nothing else, he was damned stubborn. He grabbed his crutches, took a deep breath and moved quickly and efficiently to his door. He didn't expect to see Dani anytime soon, but that didn't stop him from looking around the corners to see if she was close by. He made his way onto the deck and took a seat in the morning sunshine. On the far side, a long buffet was set up, but he wasn't sure he was up to carrying a tray and using only one of his crutches. He'd seen lots of guys do it, but he hated the thought of being the one who fell flat on his face—or rather, fell flat on his eggs. Maybe he should've brought the wheelchair after all.

George appeared at his side. "Aaron, go get in line and pick out what you want, and I'll carry the tray for you."

"I was watching the other guys and how they manage to carry it with the crutches," he said with a dry laugh. "But I figured I'd be the first one to fall and end up wearing breakfast instead."

"The thing to remember around here is, you're not likely to be the first to do anything," George said with a big grin on his face. "Takes time to learn some of these tricks. Let's head over. First you eat. Then we can do a couple runs with empty trays, and then try it with a cup of coffee and a treat, before attempting the full shebang."

That was a hell of a good idea.

Slowly the two of them made their way across the space to the buffet where George picked up a tray and a plate, then poured a cup of coffee. Together they walked along, Aaron making his choices. George never cheated him once on portions. "How can the center afford to feed all these people an unlimited amount of food three times a day?"

"Eating right is a huge part of healing," George said firmly.

As they arrived close to the end of the line, he was surprised to see somebody making smoothies behind the counter. "What are in those?"

"Very healthy stuff. How do you feel about kale, whey powder, and fresh fruit with a whole pile of other stuff in there?"

"Not as bad as I expected," he said with a smile. With George carrying the laden tray, they made their way back to the table in the sunshine. Aaron kept his gaze on the deck, working carefully around the gaps between the planks. They reached the table, and George placed the tray on its surface. Aaron glanced up to grab the back of his chair.

He froze. "Holy shit."

Levi, Aaron's older brother, and the only family he had, laughed. "Now that's a hell of a greeting, kiddo."

Aaron winced. "Please don't call me kiddo." He turned his gaze to the man beside his brother and let out a gasp of delight. "Stone?" Instantly he reached out his hand to shake Stone's. Stone and Levi had been buddies since forever, but then so had Aaron and Stone. Aaron turned to look around the common room and the deck and said, "Are you the only two here?"

"Merk and Rhodes are off on a job right now, so I dragged Stone out with us."

Just then one of the most striking blondes Aaron had ever seen arrived at his table, carrying a tray. She placed it down, reached over and kissed his cheek in the softest, gentlest way he could ever have imagined. In a voice that matched her kiss, she said, "Hi, I'm Ice."

She sat down between Levi and Stone. Both men reached over and helped themselves to items on the tray she'd brought while Aaron sat in stunned amazement. He'd heard about Ice. Hell, her reputation was well-known in military circles. Had heard the rumors about her and Levi, but Aaron had never thought he'd meet her. It wasn't like they had any kind of real familial relationship. When he regained his voice, he said quietly, "Nice to meet you, Ice."

She sent him a beautiful smile. She patted Levi's hand and said, "See? I told you we'd be welcome."

A subtle shift occurred in the table's energy. He stared down at his breakfast, his mind in turmoil, but he wouldn't waste the food. He set about eating. After a moment and several bites, he said, "Of course you're welcome. Levi's the only family I have left."

She gave Aaron a nod of approval. Damn if he didn't feel like that was something he needed. He glanced over at Levi and added, "I have no idea why you're here." Then a thought occurred. "Did Dani call you?" he asked, narrowing his eyes.

Levi gave him a blank look and said, "No, she didn't. I called her."

Aaron sat back, his stomach churning. *What had she said?* "Why would you call her?" Aaron hated the suspicions rolling through his mind, but they were there, and he was damned if he would hide them any longer. His life had been blown to shit in more ways than one. He wanted things on the table, straightforward and honest.

"Because she told me you had arrived here at her place."

"Is that why you came running here to see me? Or was it to see her?" Aaron shot his brother a quick look. He shook his head. "Part of that rings true, but the other part does not." He continued to eat while he thought about it.

"Part of it is true, yes," Levi replied quietly, "but I'd also heard rumors. Rumors I didn't like the sound of."

Aaron laid down his fork very carefully and leaned back to study his brother. "Rumors?" he asked, his voice low and hard. "What rumors?" Aaron let his gaze drift from his brother to Ice and then to Stone—both of whom were quietly eating—before zinging back to his brother.

"Rumors I never believed. That I don't like hearing. That I came to clear up."

If Aaron thought his own voice had come out hard, he'd forgotten how icy-cold his big brother could be when he was displeased. And this went well past displeased. In fact, Levi was seriously pissed.

Aaron narrowed his gaze at his brother. In a low voice, he asked, "Why are you so upset?"

"Because of the implication that you messed up."

Aaron dropped his gaze to his food and worked to control his breathing. Either that or throw a fit and send all the food on the table flying in the red haze of rage that threatened to wash over him again. When he could breathe, he realized Ice had reached across the table to lay her hand on his fists. Fists that even now were forcing the tips of his nails into the palms of his hands. Slowly he released his fingers and stretched them out.

"I did not mess up." When he could, he raised his gaze and stared at his brother, willing him to believe him. "I didn't do this."

Levi studied him for a long moment, then gave a clipped nod. "So who the hell did?"

Aaron blinked. His brother believed him. Feeling as

though a huge weight had been lifted off his shoulders, he quietly launched into an explanation of what had happened. When he finished, he studied the three faces across from him, feeling lighter than he had in months. No love was lost between him and Levi. Yet the old adage was true—blood was thicker than water. And these three were even angrier than he was.

Shocked, he realized that made him feel a whole lot better. And suddenly his appetite spiked again.

With a small smile, he picked up his fork and said, "Seeing as I can't do anything about it, what are you going to do?"

Chapter 7

HOW WERE THEY making out? The question burned inside her, but Dani deliberately avoided the deck and the breakfast buffet in order *not* to see Levi with Aaron. Would he know that the meeting was her doing? Would he hold it against her?

She bolstered herself with the thought that at least what she had done was the right thing. Even if it damaged the slow-budding relationship between the two of them. Besides, they were adults now. If he couldn't deal with this, then they had no basis for a relationship anyway. With her mind still going around and around in circles, she tried to focus on work.

Until she heard a cough in the doorway. She glanced up and blinked at the man whose broad form filled the frame.

"Levi!" She bounded off her chair, raced to the doorway and flung herself into his arms. The force of her actions sent him backward into the hallway. He laughed, picked her up, and swung her around in a huge hug. When he put her back down, she realized two other people were watching them. She flushed, but with her arm still looped around her best friend from so long ago, she grinned at the stunning Nordic-looking woman in front of her and said, "And you must be Ice."

The beautiful woman laughed and opened her arms.

"Hello, Dani. Nice to finally meet you." The two women hugged, and Dani instantly felt the connection of a potential new friend. Then her gaze landed on the big man standing behind Ice. Taller and broader than Levi.

She grinned. "Stone." She opened her arms. "Why the hell didn't you come here to recuperate? We would have had a blast together."

The big man gave a shout of laughter and picked her up in a gentle hug. She'd always been amazed that somebody so strong could be so delicate. She leaned her head back and studied his face in surprise. "You look really good." When the flush rose on his cheeks, she reached out and stroked his neck, saying, "I guess that means you have someone in your life, huh?" Stone put her down, and she stepped back slightly. "I thought you were waiting for me," she teased.

His grin widened. "No chance to duck. It hit me, and I fell bad."

"The bigger they are, the harder they fall ..." Dani looked over at Ice and grinned. "Isn't that right, Ice?"

Ice chuckled. "Certainly has been my experience."

Dani glanced around to see any sign of Aaron, but he wasn't with them. She motioned the three to follow her back into her office. "How was your reception?"

With the four of them in the room and the door closed, it was definitely crowded. She took a seat behind her desk. "I'm sorry there isn't a third chair in here."

"We're not staying anyway," Levi said.

"Oh?" She studied his face. "Did he tell you?" She sure hoped so, because she didn't want to be in the position of betraying him yet again. Some details he needed to share on his own.

"I asked around and got a lot of the details before I

showed up. Then got him to confirm them, so we have something to go on."

She nodded. "Can you do something about this?"

"We're on it."

"Good." Relief flooded her, and she smiled. "Getting to the bottom of this would be a huge comfort to him. The rumors and accusations have been eating away at him."

"It doesn't mean that the answers will make him happy. We can look into it, but there's no guarantee we can change anything," Ice warned her. "This is a sucky situation, but we'll do our best."

"I understand that." She knew all too well. "Even just that you believed him will mean a lot to him."

Levi stood. "Let's hope this has a positive effect on his mental outlook so he can heal."

Dani turned to look at Stone. "Does he know about your leg?"

Stone shrugged. "No idea."

"Do you mind if I tell him?" she asked.

"Tell him whatever you want. The sooner he comes to terms with it, the better." Stone's grin brightened his face. "It's not so bad. We're having a lot of fun with various prototypes."

"Prototypes?" she asked, fascinated. "I'm scared to ask."

Ice laughed and also rose, standing beside Levi. "It's probably a good thing if you don't. Think blue-steel, weaponized, fancy carving. One leg for Sunday outings, one for grunt work around the place, one for missions ..." She shook her head and patted Stone's arm. "I like his racer-leg the best."

"Hey, my mission leg is the coolest ever—"

"No, it's nice all right, but given the carving on the blue-steel one … particularly with the design that Lissa etched—how cool is that, to find a woman who could do such things?"

"She had no idea she could either," he admitted with a shy grin.

"What's this?" Dani asked. "Your partner does metal etching?"

"Never has before, but she's got a definite gift." He beamed. "There's also not likely to be any end of raw material for her to work on."

They had a laugh over that.

"We need to go," Levi said. "It was wonderful to see you, Dani … and thank you."

"It's lovely to see you guys," she said mistily. "I hope he doesn't hold it against me."

"I didn't tell him anything that would implicate you," Levi said. "He won't know from us."

"No, but like you, he's very intuitive, and I'm a terrible liar."

"No lying required." Ice smiled at her. "Besides, if we can help him, he should be thanking you."

"As if …" Dani's lips turned downward. "I just can't stop feeling guilty."

The other two walked out into the hallway. Levi stepped forward and lowered his voice. "You don't still have that same crush on him, do you?" he asked incredulously.

She winced. "Not really. More a case of what attracted me back then is still something that attracts me now. He's a good man. I guess I like him …" She hated how her face was warm. She could only hope Levi would ignore it.

He lifted his gaze to stare behind them and then focused it on her. "Back then he was wild. He was hurting and lashing out at everyone else. It's one of the reasons why I tried to keep you away from him."

She thought about that. "Your reasons were valid. I wasn't in the best of shape myself."

"I don't know who he is now," Levi said in a low voice. "But what I saw this morning ... well, that's a man I'm proud to call my brother."

She beamed. "Thank you. That was my impression too."

She stood in the doorway and watched as they left. She was sad to see them go. They'd been great friends once, but their lives had split and gone in different directions. Nice to know they still liked each other as adults. She was so happy Levi had found Ice. They were perfect. They looked like an all-powerful Viking couple from days gone by.

She turned in the direction of Aaron's room. Should she find him or wait? Knowing it was cowardly, she stepped back into her office. She would see him eventually. Now, with a happy heart, she finally dove into the work awaiting her.

HAD HIS BROTHER only left two hours ago? His physio had been absolutely bone-chilling, as if he'd been worked to exhaustion and then tossed into the river to fend for himself. Every muscle ached—his body was soaked in sweat, and he was so damned hot he didn't know what to do. Shane, his physiotherapist, said, "Pool, then a massage."

"Pool?" Good Lord, he hadn't seen anything close to that here. He brightened at the thought. He was so damned hot he wanted to fall in right now.

Shane laughed. "Absolutely. Let's go." He motioned at the wheelchair, and Aaron collapsed into it gratefully. Shane grabbed towels from a nearby shelf, dumping them in Aaron's lap, and then wheeled Aaron into the hall and then the elevator.

"Is the pool inside or outside?"

"Both."

Aaron raised an eyebrow at that, but he was delighted to hear it. He'd been a huge swimmer years ago. In the military, he'd always excelled at all water activities. That was one of the reasons he'd become a SEAL. It was just his thing.

They traveled down to the level below the veterinarian clinic. Shane opened the double doors to a massive walkout basement, where a large portion of the pool was inside and huge doors opened up to the outside.

"Jesus, this is incredible."

"A lot of money has been spent in making this the best place it can be," Shane said quietly. "This pool alone was a huge chunk of change." He wheeled Aaron to the men's changing room and opened the door, calling out as he went in, but it was empty. He pushed him in farther and dumped the towels to the side. He walked over to another rack, picked up a couple pairs of swim trunks and brought them over to Aaron.

"Put on the one that suits you the best, and that'll be yours to wear while here, so it goes back to your room with you. Get changed and come out on your own." Then he walked out, but just before he closed the door behind him, he said, "I'll be waiting here for you."

Still hot, but knowing that the cool, refreshing water was waiting for him, Aaron struggled into the pair he hoped would fit. He tied up the decorative front laces and then wheeled himself to the door. The double doors opened automatically, making it that much easier for him.

He found Shane already in the water. He swam over to the side and said, "Can you get in on your own?" After the morning he'd run him through, Aaron wasn't sure he could do anything. His leg felt more like butter than a body part. It was a challenge, but he was damned if he would give in that easy.

"As long as I don't have to do anything with style, I can get in." He locked the wheels of the wheelchair right beside the railing, put down his good leg and stood. Two hops and he was in the pool. As the cool water closed over his head, he almost moaned with joy. No matter what they had put him through this morning, this was worth it. Maybe this wouldn't be such a bad place to stay after all.

Chapter 8

WHEN SHE COULDN'T stand it any longer, Dani finally forced herself from her office and made her way to Aaron's bedroom, only to stare at the empty space. She shook her head. After spending the whole morning avoiding rushing to see how he was, now that she finally got up the courage, he wasn't even here. She'd consulted his timetable, but someone had made a change. As was their right, depending on what they were working on. Sometimes the patients just needed to get out of their rooms for a change of scenery.

She headed to the cafeteria. It was a bit early, but there was a chance he'd gone to eat.

Appetites ran the length of the spectrum with their patients. Sometimes they couldn't get full, and sometimes they couldn't even eat.

No sign of him. She made her way to the big deck but again nothing. The pool was on the other side. She didn't think he'd be ready for that yet, but she heard voices coming from that direction.

She snagged a coffee and then carried it to the far side of the deck where it overlooked the pool and the patio below. There he was in the water, kicking out strongly, with a bit of rock 'n' roll movement to his body. He was having a little trouble staying in a straight line, but he was doing fine. She walked down the stairs and sat down on the patio. She might as well enjoy being outside. She hadn't been in the pool herself for weeks, and that was sad.

She watched as he did several laps. When he finally stopped, he stood and brushed the water back from his head, and she could tell how happy he was. He turned his face to the sun, letting the rays beat down on his dripping features. Now *that* was the Aaron she used to know. Fun-loving, happy-go-lucky, flirty. Even with his eyes closed, he was a hell of a man. Then he opened them and gazed straight at her. She jumped. When she got ahold of herself again, she said, "How's the water feel?"

"Gorgeous. You should come in."

Not a hint of anger or annoyance in his tone. So he wasn't angry with her? That was a good sign. "Can't today—too much work for me to do."

He scoffed. "You can come in anytime you want to."

In truth, she could, but she rarely did. It wasn't that she didn't like the water, but it wasn't her first instinct when shaking loose the stress and turmoil of her day. She'd head to the horses every time.

He swam to the side of the pool near where she sat and folded his arms atop the tiled deck.

She picked up her cup and said, "If I'd known you were down here, I would have brought coffee."

"I would've enjoyed it," he said with a smile. A companionable silence hung around for a moment, until he said, "Did you phone Levi?"

She started. "Levi called me." That, at least, was the truth.

Aaron stared at the tiles and brooded.

"How did the visit go?" she asked quietly.

He shrugged. "Levi's different."

"It's been ten years. We're all different," she said drily.

He looked up at her and nodded. "I definitely am."

"Maybe that's a good thing. Maybe everybody can get along now."

He raised an eyebrow at that but didn't say anything. "It's just that the timing is odd."

Her heart sank. She wouldn't be able to get away from this. "Odd, how?" she asked in a cool voice. She picked up her cup of coffee and took a sip, staring out at the fields of green grass and white fences. This area was particularly lush-looking, and she appreciated the beauty of it.

"I tell you about my problems, and the next thing I know, big brother's racing in to help."

She froze. Then she swiveled her gaze to stare right at him. "Levi came to help?" She placed her cup down and leaned forward eagerly. "Is there anything he can do?"

"I don't know. He's making some inquiries for me." Just then Shane called from behind Aaron.

Feeling like she'd been given a reprieve, Dani picked up her now-empty cup and said, "Well, coffee break's over. I'm heading back up. It looks like you have more work to do." At his groan, she forced a light laugh and said, "You know you love this."

"Certainly more here than I did before." He dove under the water and headed toward Shane.

She watched his powerful muscles bunching naturally in the water. He had an affinity for swimming—she could tell. The rest of his body was lean, and that was what counted. Scars covered his back, and she could see where some of the muscles had atrophied. She knew swimming would help strengthen his whole body. As she watched from the stairs,

Shane went over some stroke techniques to work Aaron's back. She almost felt sorry for him. He would be sore tonight. Then again, if what he said was true, he would welcome it. Most of the injured military guys who came here, needing help, were grateful at the end of a workout. If nothing else, it gave them an outlet for all the stress and frustration they had gone through. A whole lot of things were worse than that.

Happier now that he didn't appear to hold a grudge against her, she headed back to work. He wasn't the only one needing help.

She had several other patients coming in for various issues over the next couple of months. Of course she was expecting dozens all the time. But she had no set schedule months out. Too much depended on the patients' conditions.

She was looking forward to having these three men as they could be great cheerleaders for each other. Three men— good friends—had been injured in Afghanistan—Brock Gorman, Cole Muster and Denton Hamilton and Elliot Carver was a part of the same group but wouldn't be ready to come to her center for months. They'd all known each other, but they'd been over there at different times. One had coverage but would need a boost, one had zero coverage, and she was trying to find some grant money for him. And for the third, she'd been approached by somebody else to pay for his stay. She still had a lot of work to do before it was possible to bring in the men. She idly wondered if Aaron knew any of the three. It might make him feel better to know he had friends here, all struggling to get back to their former physical selves.

Sometimes friends helped each other, but there were also

times when a patient wanted to suffer alone so no one would see them—so they wouldn't appear weak. At times though, there was just no hiding it. For some, it was important to keep that strong-man image. Sometimes having friends around bolstered that desire to stay strong while the injured man tried to hide from his friends how much he was suffering.

She pulled out their files and took a closer look. She had a couple people she could call on to see if anybody wanted to make a charitable donation. Brock looked to be the closest fit, as he already had some coverage. She picked up the phone and called Morgan Hennessy. In his eighties, Morgan had always helped out in the past. That didn't mean he would this time, but he'd been injured himself in the military, and nobody had helped him back then. He was now a wealthy philanthropist, and he was a godsend when she was in need. She smiled as he answered the phone and said in a warm voice, "Hi, Morgan. It's Dani …"

INSTEAD OF TIRING him out, the swimming invigorated him. Aaron's back muscles were responding even better than expected. It had taken a lot to press them into service, but now, even though he was shaky at the edge of the pool, he felt damned good.

Staring down at his stump as it hung over the edge, he realized he had so much to be grateful for. For some reason, that deadly cycle of his big ball of anger and self-pity over the last few months was easing.

He was glad those two emotions were not who he was. He wasn't sure what was different now, but something had shifted. Then he realized it wasn't about who he wanted to be but was about his brother—seeing his brother and realizing Levi had believed his story. That Levi would make some inquiries on Aaron's behalf made all the difference. As if Aaron could stand taller, stand straighter, as if finally his words were deemed the truth by somebody whose voice counted.

He stared across the beautiful pool, wondering when he'd realized Levi meant that much to him. Aaron should have reached out himself. Typical though, Levi had connected instead. Aaron idly wondered again if Dani had something to do with bringing Levi to the center today. As Aaron stared at his surroundings, feeling a sense of hope inside for the first time, well, he felt so damned good right now it would be hard to be upset.

Maybe he didn't need to pressure Dani about Levi. She'd seemed fairly natural in her responses. At times he was still surprised to see that she lived, worked and spent her spare hours here. Amazing how time had moved on, and she'd found what appeared to be her calling. Aaron had also seen her father running around at various times, now a beaming benevolent man. Aaron remembered hearing from others at the center about her father's history and how he'd started this place, so Aaron could imagine Dani had been involved from the ground up.

Funny, he didn't know much about Dani's father when they were younger. Although he remembered something about him being hurt and Dani struggling. He thought she'd planned to go to college but couldn't remember for what. You'd think he would remember, as everything else about her was stuck in his head. Then again school hadn't been important to him back then. In any way, shape or form. All he wanted to do was get through it the best he could and as fast as possible.

When he'd been accepted into the military, his life had started. Of course the military had also brought his life to a grinding halt a decade later. He stared down at his hands. Maybe trauma was like that—he'd hit a wall, and everything stopped. Once he realized he was being blamed and that nobody believed him, all his defenses went up, and he had locked himself inside.

"Hey, what are you doing? Sleeping here?" Shane asked, standing beside him. "Shower time. Then it's off to lunch and I promised you a massage."

"Both sound great." Using the railing he hopped up on one foot, then he turned and looked around, but his wheelchair was pulled back a few feet, out of the way of people walking around the pool. He had no crutches, not to mention the tiles were now wet from where he'd been sitting, all the way to where Shane now stood. Aaron motioned at the crutches and asked, "Shane, can you pass me those?"

Instead, with a big grin on his face, Shane said, "Here, use my arm and step." He reached out a thick forearm for Aaron to use as balance as he took two hops to the wheelchair before moving smoothly into the showers.

By the time he was done and dressed and heading back out the door, he could feel the fatigue setting in. Not that it mattered because his appetite was even bigger, raging to be fed now. So food first, then a massage in bed. He'd be asleep in no time. With a sense of satisfaction at his morning, he headed off to do just that.

Chapter 9

B Y THE TIME the dinner buffet was setting up, Dani felt good about her day. She'd made great inroads into her paperwork. She'd contacted several benefactors and had already received enough to cover the three men at the top of her list.

Tossing down her pen, she decided that was enough for the day. She got up and exited her office, closing and locking the door behind her. In the hallway, she stood and studied the activity around her. There'd been no major upsets for a couple of weeks now, and a general air of peace and contentment filled the center. It was all good.

"Dani, got time for dinner with your old man?" Her father ambled toward her, with a big lazy grin on his face.

She beamed. "Best offer I've had all day."

He hooked his arm through hers and gently led her toward the dining hall. She didn't always eat here. Many times she preferred to go home, but she knew her dad wanted to be here. Dinner was likely to be a catch-up session on shoptalk, but that was their relationship these days, and she hadn't had a good discussion with him for a long time.

The dining area was busy, but the two of them could always find a place in the far corner if they wanted it. She sometimes felt guilty about keeping a table just for them when she only used it maybe half the time, but it was important for her to know she and her father always had a spot to meet and eat. He seemed to be perfectly content to live most of his life down here. He was well-known to the staff and had lots of friends among the patients. Those he didn't know he made friends with very quickly.

But instead of serving themselves right away, he wanted to sit and talk over coffee first. While she was happy to visit with her dad, she wondered if something else was going on.

"So how are the newest arrivals doing?" he asked with a smile.

She narrowed her gaze at him. "As far as I know, everyone's settling in nicely," she said smoothly. "Anyone in particular you're asking about?" But she knew. Of course she knew.

"I understand that Aaron, Levi's younger brother, is doing better."

She felt his aging blue gaze pierce her. "Yes, he is." She laughed quietly. "I'm surprised you didn't bring it up earlier."

"I was waiting for you to say something about it," he said, leaning back with a twinkle in his eye. "So how is he? You had quite the thing for him way back when."

"I did not," she protested. "I might have had a *little* thing for him back then, but it wasn't that bad. He was just so ... larger than life."

He snickered. "This is somebody who watched you go through years of that sideways look, flushes and giggles, and moody staring into the middle of nowhere," he said. "Allow me to now hold a different opinion on that."

She rolled her eyes. "Whatever. Your memory is obviously a little bit lacking."

He chuckled. "I thought I saw Levi come through this

place this morning, but I can't be sure because, boy, that man is a far cry from the kid who used to hang around the house all the time."

"It was Levi. You didn't see much of him toward the end, when he headed into the military, but he's definitely the same person. He came to visit his brother."

"Good. Family should stick together."

After that, things returned to more mundane business about finances, and she told him about Morgan donating money to help a couple more people get the treatment they needed.

He beamed. "We need more people like him," he said. "Many people are in need."

"Even if we had all the money in the world, we wouldn't be able to help them all," she said. "We have to be realistic. We'll help those who we can."

"Who's coming next then?" he asked. He picked up his cup of coffee and sipped it, staring at her over the rim. "You know how I like to know who's coming in."

She shook her head. "You're just seeing how many more friends you can make out of the new patients. Soon, but no idea how soon will be Brock Gorman, Cole Muster and Denton Hamilton and hopefully Elliot Carver. The first three need financial assistance."

He frowned. "What's happened to the insurance companies these days?"

"The military is handling Denton, but he's not quite ready to travel, and Brock has a lot of medical insurance but not quite enough to cover our place," she admitted. "But with Morgan covering the balance for Brock and all of Cole's fees, we should have all three men in soon. They were in the same arm of the military, and they know each other. I was hoping that being here with friends would help them push each other into better circumstances."

"I agree, in theory, but we don't have three empty beds, do we?"

She shook her head. "No. I have one. I'm working on getting Brock's travel arrangements completed first, since he can essentially move in at any time. We also have someone releasing next week, so in theory, we could take Cole too. But as far as Denton is concerned, we could be looking sometime weeks away."

"Have you considered bringing in more staff?"

"I don't have much choice, seeing as Susie and Dennis handed in their notices." She propped her chin on her palm and rested her elbow on the table. "Susie's returning to school."

"Why is Dennis leaving?" her dad grumbled. "I really like that man."

She chuckled at her father's indignation. "Because he and Susie are an item, and she's attending school in California. They aren't willing to be apart."

"Damn." He stared off in the distance. "Is she picking up skills we can use later?"

"Absolutely. Physiotherapy."

"Before they leave, make sure they know they are welcome back."

"Yes, Dad," she replied drily. He meant well, but he said the same damned thing every time they had a similar situation. "I doubt it will happen, knowing Susie's family is back west, so ..." She glanced at the buffet line and noticed it had shortened. "Are we planning on talking the whole night or getting something to eat too?" she asked, teasing.

He bounced to his feet. For somebody who'd been

through all the health issues he had, he moved very quickly. They were soon standing at the buffet and serving themselves some delicious-looking grilled salmon. By the time Dani had filled a plate and headed to their table, the smell reminded her just how absolutely empty her stomach was. As she sat down, she said, "I don't think I've eaten all day."

Her father raised his gaze. "What? You have to start looking after yourself." He lifted his fork and shook it at her. "Don't make me sic the staff on you and have them remind you all the time that you can't neglect your own health."

She shuddered. "Please don't."

As they sat there, talking and enjoying dinner together, she glanced around the dining room, feeling a sense of pride in all they'd accomplished. Sure, there'd been a lot of hiccups along the way, and more hiccups could certainly appear in the future, but for the moment, things were doing rather well.

"You have a look of satisfaction on your face." Her dad's voice interrupted her musings. "What's up?"

She put down her fork, and reaching across the table, laid her hand on his. "Just thinking about this special project you started way back when and how fantastic it's all turned out," she said warmly.

He laced his fingers through hers and squeezed them. "I couldn't have done it without you, girl."

"Well, it's been a team effort getting it this far."

At that they both quieted and ate their meals. It wasn't long before she stood up to head home and turned to her father. "You coming home tonight?"

"Of course I am. Just as I do every night, but in the meantime, I'll go downstairs and take a look at our four-legged patients."

She stopped gathering their dishes. "I'm out of touch today. Did we get somebody new in?"

"Well, a rosy boa who's got a way-too-long slice on its back," he said. "And we have a Maine Coon cat that looks like he's been through more than his fair share of troubles. The team'll have to work on taming him in order to change his ways, although that crippled back leg will halt his hunting days. Treatment will be difficult because he can't be touched easily." Then he gave her another bit of news. "We got a little filly in today. Less than a year old."

She raised her eyebrows at that. "Normally I know when horses are coming in. Why wasn't I told about this one?" she asked in surprise. Then shook her head. "Listen to me. Like everyone isn't run off their feet already."

"I think everybody considers this one theirs," he said with a laugh. "She's small, beautiful and loves people."

"Where is she?"

"In the back stall all by herself, but old Maggie is in the stall next door to keep her company."

"Can't she be in the same stall as Maggie?"

"She likes people, but she's not sure about other horses," her father said. "It looks like the owners kept her in the house, and so all she knows is people."

"Well, come on. Let's go see her." She hated to think of a horse being kept as a pet. They were meant to run free and to be wild. Or at least pastured where they had lots of room to move and run with other horses.

She quickly walked over to the elevators. She admitted to being a little miffed at not hearing about the horse earlier. Normally Stan would have done that right off.

When she reached the vet's office, with her dad only a step behind her, Stan was looking stressed and harried and had his hands full with a monster-size cat. Her father raced forward and grabbed a second towel to help wrap up the critter's legs.

Stan stepped back with a relieved laugh. "Good timing. This guy just about got the better of me." As it was, his arms showed signs of the cat's displeasure.

Dani walked over and gently held out a hand to the cat. With his arms and legs bundled up in the towel, he couldn't scratch her, but she wasn't sure if he wanted to be petted or if he just wanted to take off her hide. However, he accepted her caress and a quick scratch behind his ears. His eyes were still wild-looking, but he was calming down.

"What's wrong with him?" she asked.

"Broken back leg that healed crooked. It's causing all kinds of damage on the joints."

"I heard that another horse was on the premises." She glanced over at Stan. "Is that true?"

He lifted his head, a confused look in his eyes. Then his gaze cleared, and he said, "Yes. I meant to let you know earlier, but my day's been like this since I first arrived."

She nodded. "I suspected as much. What's wrong with her?"

"Nothing and everything." He shook his head. "She was treated as a pet until they realized they couldn't keep it up. Her hooves are in rough shape. They are still so soft, and unfortunately one of them is cracked, so we'll work on that. She's also very skittish about other horses, having never been around them."

Dani couldn't imagine. "I'd like to see her when we're done here."

He waved her off and said, "You don't need to stay. Go down and visit her. Her name is Molly."

With a glance at her father, she smiled and left them to it. That tomcat wasn't interested in having anybody look after him, whereas Molly appeared to be very much a people-person. Dani walked to the attached stables where Maggie had her permanent home. The older horse would be close enough that Molly could see, hear and touch her on the nose, if need be, at least until they saw how Molly handled being with another horse. Dani came around the corner to look into Molly's stall and spotted a pair of crutches leaning against the barn door.

Her heart raced. She had deliberately avoided him all afternoon and evening, but was it possible ...? She leaned over the half-door to look in at one of the prettiest little fillies she'd ever seen. Even more heartbreaking was the sight of the big man sitting at her side, gently brushing her, with a look of absolute adoration on his face.

"Hi, Aaron. I wasn't expecting to see you here."

HEARING THE FAMILIAR voice, Aaron turned to study Dani, her gaze locked on the little horse in front of them. He remembered her being one of those horse-crazy girls back then. He could just imagine how this little heartbreaker would affect her. "I heard about her earlier," he confessed. "I couldn't *not* come down and see her."

"You get to spend as much time with the animals as you can manage without avoiding any treatments," she said with a laugh, not moving any farther.

"You coming in?"

"Maybe I should just leave the two of you together," she admitted. "Sometimes the animals are the best healing force we have."

"That doesn't mean there isn't enough to go around." He motioned toward the door. "Come on in and say hi. This little girl's Molly."

"How's she getting along with Maggie?"

On cue, Maggie's head popped over the side. Then she gave Molly a nicker. Molly nickered back.

Now *that* was a good sign.

He watched with joy as old Maggie gently dropped her head over the stall to make sure the little one was doing okay. Molly hobbled over to the side and leaned against the wood so Maggie could get as close as possible.

Instead of walking to Molly first, Dani headed to Maggie and gave her a good scratch and a cuddle. "You just love new ones, don't you, Maggie? The eternal mother, that's what you are."

"That's a good thing because Molly could sure use some guidance." Aaron looked at the small animal, a flash of pain crossing his face. "Whatever possesses people to treat animals as if they're humans? This horse lived in the house, going up and down stairs and had a bed."

Dani shook her head. "I can see people doing things like that when the animals are small and adorable, but very quickly it becomes impractical, and it's not healthy for the animal, never for a horse. What do you do when she reaches Maggie's age?"

"It's ridiculous."

He sat back and watched as Maggie gently cuddled with the filly. One of Molly's hooves was bandaged, and she'd need some rehab work, but she appeared to be in good health otherwise. "At least she didn't stay there very long."

"Exactly." He reached over and grabbed a crutch, and

using it as a lever, he rose. With his other crutch, he hobbled to the gate. He went to open it but found Dani there ahead of him. She opened it up for him and then followed him out, closing the door on the two animals.

"They're beautiful," she said. "Both of them."

"Especially right now. That connection. That bond. They don't care about the garbage that came with each other. They don't care about likes, dislikes, pain or fears. It's just all in the moment for them."

He felt her gaze searching his face and realized he had revealed a little too much of his personal thoughts.

"Too bad we didn't know that," she said, injecting some humor into the conversation. "All those years ago, when we knew each other. And yet, we *didn't* know each other or how much things would change since then."

"But none of it's baggage we have to bring forward."

"We're not the same people we were back then."

"True enough," he said with a note of bitterness in his voice. "No matter how much I try not to dwell on it, it's hard not to."

"Molly's lost a lot too. Just like you."

He waved an arm. "You think I don't feel guilty because I'm bitching and whining, and yet I'm so much better off than so many people? The thing is, it doesn't make it any easier. I'm still missing a leg."

"Did you know Stone's missing a leg too?"

He turned to stare at her. "What?"

She nodded. "You didn't notice it because his prosthetic limb fits so well that he moves easily. He's gotten so used to it that it almost doesn't matter to him anymore." She shrugged. "I'm sure he went through hell in the beginning. I'm sure there were long days and dark nights when he wished things were different, but he's back in action, doing exactly what he's always loved doing."

Aaron set his crutches to the side and rested his arms on the stall door. "I remember hearing something about that," he admitted. "But when I saw him, he looked so natural, so normal, that it never occurred to me. Most of the time I'm fine. It was just a leg. I can replace that if I need to. Once I get these back muscles fixed and the last couple surgeries done, I'll be good to go." He paused for a moment. "Honestly I feel more positive than I did before. A lot of that is thanks to this place, but at times, I feel the loss so much more, like I'll explode from the fallout."

"Of course you do," she said in a quiet voice. "It's important to honor that loss. But then it's just as important to pick up and move on."

"You must think I'm a fool."

She walked away, her hand reaching out to pat him on the shoulder as she went past. "No, I think you're just at a point in your life when you have to decide if you want to move on or if you want to stay stuck and wallow."

Maybe it was her words, maybe it was the note of rebuke he heard in her tone, or maybe it was the pat on the shoulder that reminded him of the last pat she'd given Maggie as she walked away, but he snapped, "I'm not a pet."

She turned and bunched her hands on her hips, glaring at him. "You certainly aren't. You're more like a caged grizzly."

He reached out and grabbed her hand, jerking her toward him, but she shook herself free from his grip and snapped, "Don't you dare!" Images of Jim flooded her brain.

"Don't I dare what?" He glared at her, then saw something in her expression. He frowned now, considering her reaction. Although, to her, right now, she probably didn't note the difference between his earlier glare and his thoughtful frown.

"Don't treat me like that." She shoved her face into his, her gaze hard. "You don't have the right to push me around."

His eyebrows rose. He hadn't done it roughly. But what he intended to do probably wasn't a good idea either. Still, her rage didn't stop him from trying. Like with any abused animal, he slowly reached out to Dani and tenderly placed a hand at the back of her neck and pulled her inexorably toward him. "I wasn't pushing you," he said softly. "I was pulling you."

When her face was right next to his, their noses almost touching and his warm breath against hers, he whispered, "I would never hurt you. I just want to kiss you." And he gently covered her mouth with his.

Chapter 10

JUST BECAUSE, DEEP inside, she had been hoping they'd get to this point didn't mean she was ready when it happened. Of course, it took a heightened event—a fight—for them to cross the line and to show their true feelings. Still, she wanted this, and she'd always been an all-or-nothing kind of girl. She threw her arms around his neck and returned his kiss.

Instantly his arms closed around her like a vise. His fingers widened on the back of her head to shift her position so he could take better possession of her mouth. Dani felt like she was drowning in joy when the sound of a cough interrupted them.

"Sorry, you two," Stan said brightly.

Instantly they broke apart.

"I should check on Molly before I hopefully go home, sometime soon."

Flushed and overheated, Dani pulled her hair back in a nervous motion. "Sorry for blocking your way. I have to get home too." She quickly brushed past the two men. Belatedly she glanced around and realized, with great relief, that her father wasn't here. If he'd come with Stan, she'd never have heard the end of it.

She kept to the less-traveled routes to the center and let herself out the back door. Well past time to go home. Her cheeks were hot and flushed from the kiss, and emotions raced through her. What had she done? Although she was blasting herself for overstepping the line, she couldn't regret the moment. Now she knew Aaron cared. Now she knew he was interested. She could work with that. She was patient. She could wait until he was ready for so much more.

She ran toward home. The sound of Midnight moving in the side paddock caught her ear. She walked over to the horse as he neared the fence, and she threw her arms around him in a big hug. This was what she needed. Her old friend. She had spent hours sharing her lost and broken loves with Midnight. Now look at her. For so long, she had been afraid she'd never find true love. Afraid it had just passed her by. She'd watched all her friends get engaged, get married and have children while Dani had had a few relationships but never found *the one*. She admitted to herself she'd worried it was too late, and she'd missed out. Maybe now she could finally have that relationship she wanted.

Instantly her critical side stepped in. *Whoa, Dani. You've been here before. You thought you had that relationship a time or two already. Take it easy. Go slow. If you're lucky, this will be your second chance with Aaron. But don't count on it. He walked out of your life ten years ago, and you didn't see him again until now. What's to stop him from walking away once he's back on his feet and healthy again? Are you prepared to give your all, only to turn around and not see him again for another ten years? If ever?*

The trouble was, she was prepared to do exactly that. But was he?

TWO GOOD LEGS would've given Aaron the same fast exit it had given Dani. Instead, he struggled to get his crutches under his arms while Stan stood nearby, grinning at him like a fool.

"Don't make too much of that," Aaron warned.

But his words went unheeded as Stan's grin widened. "How would you expect me to take it?"

Hobbling away as quickly as possible—without looking like he was escaping—Aaron threw back, "Just a kiss between old friends."

"I don't know why you'd want to fool yourself," Stan said, "but there's no way in hell *that* was between old friends. That was between new lovers. And congrats, by the way."

Aaron stopped and slowly turned to look at Stan. The man was still grinning at him. "What do you mean, congrats?"

"Dani hasn't had a relationship in over a year. Her last breakup was pretty ugly," Stan admitted. "We've all been keeping a close eye on her, but she hasn't let anybody else get close." He pointed at Aaron and said, "You're the first one. So you can bet we'll be watching."

"So then, what's with that congrats?" Aaron said drily. "It sounds more like a warning to me than a wish of good fortune."

"It's only a warning to treat her right," Stan said quietly. "Her heart is solid gold, and she's helped a ton of people here."

Aaron studied the older man's face and nodded.

He'd turned to leave again when Stan called back, "Did I hear something about you'd planned on being a vet?"

Aaron snorted. "I see the rumor mills are just as bad here as they are elsewhere."

"Worse," Stan said cheerfully. "But, if that's true, do you want to help down here sometimes? I could really use it."

Aaron laughed wryly. "So it's not about whether I was interested at one time in being a vet but more of whether I would volunteer now."

"Both work for me if I get some extra help." Stan shrugged. "These animals need love and attention. I only have so many hours in a day."

"Don't patients upstairs come down to help out?"

"Patients and staff," Stan said. "Of course it's a mutually beneficial arrangement."

"So you still need more people, or are you just offering me something to do with my time while I'm here?"

Maybe his tone had come out a little too harsh because Stan leaned against Molly's stall door and crossed his arms over his chest. "So don't come." He shrugged. "No real skin off my nose. But anybody who's watched you with the animals can see how much they affect you. So I guess it's not an olive branch but an invitation. If you'd like to spend time with them, then do. If you don't want to, then don't." Stan gave him curt nod of dismissal and walked into the stall to check on Molly.

Aaron hesitated. He'd let his irritation get the better of him. And felt like a heel. Just because he had his issues didn't mean he could snap at everybody. He thought about apologizing to Stan and then wondered if not better just to let things lie. Depressed again and hating that sensation of having done wrong, he started to leave. Something he'd been trying to do for the last ten minutes. But then his conscience prodded him, and he couldn't let things end on this note.

He turned and hobbled toward the stall door. Quietly he watched as Stan checked over the little filly and then put his arms around her to hold and to pat her. The filly buried her face into him and nudged him with her big nose.

It was a special moment. One Aaron was glad to see. Because Stan was right. Aaron did love animals. Abruptly he blurted out, "I'm sorry."

A look of surprise on his face, Stan turned toward him. "No need to apologize. I understand. If it will make you feel any better, this place is full of other people who have been wounded in more ways than one. The animals help. If you already have an affinity for our furry friends in the first place, it's not a bad way to train for a new career."

Aaron winced. "That's a lot of years."

"Were you planning on doing anything else during that time?"

He'd heard similar lines before from various people but this time it struck home. "I do have a Bachelor of Science degree," he said quietly. "I've never applied to vet school."

"When, and if, you're ever ready to take that step, we'll write a reference letter for you," Stan said with a smile. "God knows we could use another vet around here." He straightened and faced Aaron. "When you're more mobile, I could use an assistant too."

"That's a very generous offer."

"I can train somebody to do the work I need done. I can't train anybody to have the same affinity with horses and other animals that you do. That's a natural gift you have. Something you should be proud of."

"It would be nice to be proud of something," Aaron replied drily. "When life kicks the shit out of you, it's good to find something to help hold you up."

Stan grinned. "I don't know your story, and you don't have to tell me, but I do understand the man who stands in front of me. So, whatever the hell is bothering you, you either need to fix it or move past it. A whole life out there is waiting for you."

On that note, Stan exited the stall, secured the door and headed toward the outdoor exit. He gave Aaron a brief wave. "See you tomorrow."

Aaron made his way upstairs with Stan's words ringing in his ears. Was it even possible to consider his suggestion? It would be a long commitment, but would that matter when it was something Aaron had always loved and had hoped to do? He'd turned his back on that dream to go into the military. To follow Levi's steps and to prove he was as good as his brother. Aaron had taken to the career well. But life was different now, and it was time to bring out the other dreams and to see if they still held the same magic.

He stared down at where his leg used to be and realized that many of his issues were more mental blocks than anything else. Nothing was stopping him from leading a more fulfilling life. It was all about his mindset, his attitude. If he could deal with those, going back to school would be an option ... or rather it might be a necessity, given the fact he had to create a second career for himself now.

So why not become a vet? Why not make one of his biggest dreams come true? Of course his mind immediately jumped to another dream he'd had for years.

Was it possible that after all this time a relationship with Dani could come true too?

Chapter 11

THE NEXT SEVERAL days and the following weeks settled into a routine. Dani stopped by to see Aaron in the mornings when she first arrived, spending a few minutes laughing and joking with him, before heading to her office. Out of habit, she would check to see where he was and what he was up to at lunchtime. Sometimes they connected to sit together and eat, and sometimes it didn't work out. But, as the days slipped by, she realized just how much their moments together meant. She'd catch herself staring into space with a silly smile, thinking about him, completely ignoring the work in front of her. Like now. She gave her head a shake and laughed. "It's like you're a damned teenager again, girl."

Her father popped his head into her office and studied her face. "Glad to see you looking so happy today. Can you share the joy?"

She grinned. "No way. I get enough teasing around here as it is."

"So does this have something to do with Aaron?" he asked with a chuckle. "All the wagging tongues say so."

"So I hear," she said. "Maybe it's just nice to spend time with an old friend."

Dad walked in and sat down in the spare chair. "Hardly an old friend, my dear. An old flame maybe."

"No, a crush. He never got to the flame part, remember?"

"That's because you were hanging around Levi so much. I bet Aaron hated that. Probably figured you were his brother's girl. Nothing like jealousy to come between siblings."

"He barely knew I existed," she said, shaking her head. "Besides, that was a long time ago." Truthfully she knew he had liked her a little back then. Over the last few weeks, they had talked every day, and she had to admit to loving the blossoming relationship.

The only dark spot was the lack of any follow-up on Levi's part. Her hand itched to pick up the phone and call him, but she held back. He'd call her when he knew something and was ready to share.

In the meantime, Aaron had made tremendous progress. She'd originally booked him for six months at Hathaway, but she didn't think he would need all that time. At that thought, the corners of her mouth turned down. She had no idea what she would do when he left. It was a good thing—he would be able to move on, but what would that life entail? And maybe more importantly to her, who would he move on with?

"Have you discussed his future with him?" her father asked curiously. His head tilted slightly, as if he'd get a better view of her reaction that way.

She cast her gaze to her cluttered desktop and shook her head. "No. It's too soon."

"No, it's not," he said with a smile. He stood and added, "It's never too early for something like that."

Walking toward the door, Dad turned and said in a quiet voice, "Loving Aaron will never be easy. He's a complex, difficult man, who has a lot of issues from his military years and who now sees himself as less than complete. Even when he gets his prosthesis and is fully functioning, even with his back fixed, he'll never feel like he's whole. It'll take a lot of effort on your part to make him feel that way." He hesitated. "Just make sure you're ready to take that step. It could take him years to get over what he's been through. He might never overcome his wartime experiences."

She understood where Dad was coming from. He had been there himself. And he cared. She smiled warmly at him. "It *will* take years for him," she said. "That's okay because I have years of experience here and a lot more years of personal experience with you."

A chagrined look came over his face. He scuffed his shoes on the floor as he shoved his hands into his pockets and said, "I guess I was quite a trial, wasn't I? I'm sorry about that."

Dani rose and rushed to him, almost knocking her chair down in the process. "Don't think that. Never. It was a difficult time for you. The worst part for me was feeling so helpless. All I could do was lend emotional support or hopeful words, encouragement."

He reached out and hugged her gently. "You did a damned good job. I hope Aaron won't need as much for as long. He's a young man, and he's healing beautifully. I'm sure he'd heal that much faster with a lovely young woman at his side. I just don't want you to get hurt again."

She looked up into his eyes and said, "I don't want that either. But I think it's too late. I already love him." Quiet for a long moment, she added wistfully, "Maybe I always have."

ONCE AGAIN, THE days fell into a simple pattern—therapy, lunch with Dani, exercise, more therapy, and then, if Aaron was lucky, he caught a glance of her at the end of her day. If he was even luckier, he got to spend the evening down with Stan in the vet clinic and with Dani herself.

They fell into an easy camaraderie. Something was developing that was precious. Something beyond his expectations. Something that was beyond what he'd hoped for. What he thought couldn't happen in his life anymore. His world had been so black. He'd been so full of loss and anger and grief that he hadn't seen there was light. That there were people who didn't care about his leg, or his disability, or the fact that he wasn't as strong and big and healthy as he used to be. She had known him back then. She knew him now. Apparently, she still liked him. How lucky was he?

He still had lots of questions about being with her. There was also fear. What if he didn't like those answers? He didn't want to push it. An idyllic bubble was surrounding them right now, and for once, he didn't want to blow that. Fantasies were only possible as long as one could still believe. Reality was going be a bitch, if it turned out to be something different.

He could feel himself getting stronger, day-by-day. A little more adept—a little more comfortable with the reality of crutches and wheelchairs. At that thought, he laughed.

Dani was walking at his side as they headed toward the pool, and she smiled and said, "It's nice to hear your laughter, but what was that all about?"

He explained. "The new leg alone was interesting. I can see unlimited potential for design creativity, to make these legs a work of art. I used to do metalwork way back when in high school." He remembered that he'd loved it.

She cast a look at him and said, "I remember you brought home a candleholder or something one time, and it broke."

He stopped and stared at her as the memory slammed into his mind. He laughed again. "Okay, so maybe I wasn't so good at metal art, but I enjoyed it."

After his swim, they headed outside to where the horses were. Molly was in the pasture with Stan. Her hoof was healing, but she was confused by fences and by the different bushes in the paddocks. Aaron still couldn't believe somebody had kept a horse in a house. What was wrong with people?

"She is beautiful," Dani said happily. "I'm so glad that when we first converted this place just for Dad's recuperation, we kept the space for the animals intact."

He turned to look at her. "How did that come about?" He waved an arm and said, "It's a great pairing, but at the same time, not exactly what most people would think to do."

"It was a former veterinary school, which offered very specialized training. The doctors and residents were housed upstairs, and a full veterinarian clinic, including a surgery ward, was on the main floor." She turned to look at the buildings and fields around them. "When it closed and fell into disrepair, the property dropped in value. At the time, my father was desperately in need of something to help him through his pain, his loss and he bought it. Because the upstairs was easier for him to navigate, he set up in one room and brought in physiotherapy on a regular basis. A local vet asked about using the existing facilities for his practice, which started the animal side of things. The vet worked downstairs, and the animals came and went on a regular basis. Then two of dad's cronies moved in, and the physiotherapy part increased, and it just evolved from there."

"It's nice to see what you started with grew into a business with your own two hands."

"Actually it snowballed," she confessed. "Luckily Gram was here for him at the time as I was studying business. Each week when I came to see how Dad was doing, I realized this place had changed him, given him a whole new lease on life. Plus, he was getting stronger physically. I decided to stay and commit myself to the project with him. Now look at the place," she said with a big smile.

"It's pretty amazing," Aaron said. "I'd love to have been a part of this. Of the development and construction."

"There were days, weeks, where I didn't think we'd make it."

"It's not just a business—you're helping people, and you're helping animals." He turned, leaning his back against the rails, and stared up at the massive two-storied facility. "You even have room to expand, if you need to."

She laughed wryly. "I'm not sure I could handle much more."

A waft of warm air hit the back of Aaron's neck. He turned to look at Maggie behind him. He reached up a hand and gently caressed the older mare. "The animals need help just as much as people. Your place here is massive."

"Yes, it is." She studied the building. "Dad's responsible for bringing in some of the modern facilities, like the pool, and the handicap ramps and rails. Everybody deserves a chance to heal in whatever way they require."

He nodded and gave her a small smile. "Well, I do appreciate it."

She smiled back, slipping her arm through his, and said,

"Good. How about we get a cup coffee before I head to my place?"

"How about we take that coffee and go to your place?" he said with a laugh, knowing it wasn't possible, might never be.

She grinned. "Wishful thinking on your part, mister. No undercover activities for you for quite a while." She gave him a comic leer.

He chuckled, relieved to see he could joke about the subject. "Undercover? I don't think I've ever heard it referred to in that way before." He rolled it around on his lips and said, "But I do like it."

"What, the activities or the word?" she teased.

He leaned in and kissed her gently on the cheek. "Both."

She smiled and kissed him directly.

With the sun going down and his heart hammering against his chest, this was as poignant as it was beautiful. He reached up to cup her face. He turned her slightly and kissed her properly. Deeply. Passionately.

When she responded with a fiery heat of her own, he spun just enough to pin her against the fence, his body holding her captive in his arms. He shared a little of his passion. If she had any idea how much he wanted her, she'd run for the hills. As she met him kiss for kiss, as her arms reached up and around his neck to hold him close while her hips pressed tight against his, he realized she was a perfect match for him in every way.

Then he felt something else. Something he hadn't felt in a very long time. He withdrew his lips and crushed her against his chest. He'd been afraid for so long his body had forgotten how to make love. Maybe he was injured to a point where the doctors hadn't even been aware. Like something was wrong with him mentally or physically or emotionally, and therefore, he'd never make love to someone again. But the proof was in his arms as his body responded in the most satisfying way.

Overwhelmed, he buried his face against her neck and just held her close.

Chapter 12

WAS HE CRYING? She wasn't sure what was going on, but something major was breaking for him. He held her so tight, as if he would never let her go. She reached up to stroke his cheek, and sure enough, she felt wetness at the corners of his eyes. That made her heart ache all the more for him. She wrapped her arms around him and hugged him close. Finally he regained some control and released her. He stepped back slightly, a bit of a cocky smile on his lips, and leaned on the fence. "Sorry. That went a little further than I intended."

She smiled up at him. "Nice to know that much passion is on the inside." She reached out and stroked his bottom lip.

"Hey, that's my line," he said with a smile. "If I ever get out of that hospital bed permanently, you know what's coming."

"When you leave that hospital bed," she teased, "you know exactly where I live." She patted his cheek. "It will be months yet as nothing should distract you or slow down your healing process. And on that note," she added, "I'll head to my cabin." She reached up and brushed a gentle kiss across his lips, then turned and left him staring after her.

It was a beautiful evening, but she had shivers racing up and down her arms, which she tucked against her chest to hide. She just needed a few minutes alone. The passion they had shared took her by surprise and frankly shook her to her core. She'd always thought they'd be explosive if they ever got together. Yet, she'd never expected them to be a couple, so she hadn't had any real hope of that evolving. Now it was all she could think about.

She was sure she wouldn't get any sleep tonight. That man was lethal. And she couldn't be happier. She'd also felt his response to her and had wondered if that had been part of his overwhelming emotion. One day he might tell her. In the meantime, she'd do what she'd always done and just accept every step of progress he made with gratefulness.

She wasn't a prude, and she'd been through enough herself. She also knew she couldn't just go to bed with somebody without caring, without that emotional connection. She'd been there, done that and regretted every last minute. But she'd also been to bed with men who she had thought were forever, and that hadn't worked out so well either.

As a young girl, a teenager on the brink of womanhood, she'd attended all the parties and get-togethers where everyone went for the easy sex. That was the reason she'd ended up with Levi. He'd been interested, but she hadn't been, not in that way, and somehow they'd still remained friends—a friendship that had lasted as he went through several girlfriends over time. He'd watched her go through half as many boyfriends.

She'd been a good girl—the sweet, simple innocent girl on the block. Growing up, Gram had been the strict moral influence in her life with black-and-white views of what was right and what was wrong. Dani had been terrified of having sex because of Gram. It took Dani a long time to take that step. She figured Gram was watching over her and would poke her in the ribs—like she used to all the time—and say, "Stop that!"

On the other hand, Aaron had been a party animal. That had never appealed to her. She had been raised differently. But coming of age with two very sexual males, Aaron and Levi, had been an alluring temptation to change her way of life. Still, she knew better. The only way to protect herself was to back off and shut down that part of her. It had worked well.

She went to college and found someone she cared for, and she thought that was it. They had a year-long relationship, and, just when she thought he would ask her to marry him, he broke it off instead.

She'd been devastated. It was a hard lesson, but one she'd learned from, and she went on to several other relationships. Another one almost ready for that wedding ring. Her father had hated that man—Jim. Dad had tried so hard to stop her from marrying the wrong man.

She wondered if she was just getting too old for relationships. "On the shelf," as her grandmother would've said. Maybe she needed to just accept her life as it was. She shook her head. Like hell she did.

Aaron had always been the one who made her pulse jump. When he walked into a room, she lost the ability to speak coherently. Levi had laughed at her. The last thing he'd wanted was her hooking up with his playboy brother. So he'd done his best to keep them apart. Maybe that had been a good thing. Back then, it wouldn't have been so sweet. But now she wasn't that same foolish girl, and Aaron was no longer the playboy, and she really liked what she had discovered about him.

She was glad they'd had these months together, getting

reacquainted. They would have been more perfect if Levi had found something about Cain. Dani believed it was a necessary step for Aaron's healing. She just didn't know how Aaron would react if there was no happy ending. Would it keep him down for the rest of his life, or would he finally put the past behind him and move on?

Heavy questions. She knew from her own experience that men dissatisfied with life became very difficult over time. That was why Jim had gotten more and more abusive. It had started out small, with just insults and comments about not looking after herself, or not wearing makeup and not caring enough to pretty herself up for her man.

She shook her head at the hard memories. Now she knew he'd simply been grooming her to accept even worse treatment down the road—because, of course, it had gotten worse. Much worse. At that time, she was working at the center full-time, and Jim was a mainstay here. Everybody else wasn't happy about their relationship, but very few said anything to her about it. When some did, she didn't welcome their criticism. Of course she didn't—she was in a relationship, looking forward to getting married and maybe starting that family she wanted.

The abuse had worsened. A couple people told him off, and Jim got belligerent and ugly. He had his revenge in private. He'd been living with her, in her house, for six months. She hadn't realized just how much the stress had affected her until her father took her to one side and said she had to stop.

"Don't you see what's happening to you? You've lost weight. You're jumpy and timid. You're easily startled. A door slams, and you're ready to break apart." Dad shook his head and wrapped his arms around her. "Dani, I love you. I can't stand to see you tortured this way. Get rid of him."

"It's not that bad," Dani whined.

"How bad does it have to get?" her father snapped. "He beats you, and the next time he could kill you." He shook his head. "I've already lost your mother. I couldn't lose you too—and never that way."

At that point she could see the fissures in Jim's personality. Then they quickly became major cracks. She just didn't know how to heal them. She had tried to explain this to her father, but he'd been adamant.

"There is no healing this. It will just get worse."

She looked back over that long year and had finally become aware of the slow and insidious increase in abuse, which she'd learned to accept. Then came the final straw for her. They'd had a fight. A huge fight. He'd beaten her thoroughly this time. When he stormed out of the house that night, he had tossed all kinds of insults at her. She picked up the phone and called 9-1-1, asking for both an ambulance and the sheriff, and finally called her father.

Jim remained in jail, somewhere in the middle of the country. She hoped he never came back. She'd done everything she could to make sure he stayed where he was for as long as possible.

Thankfully he hadn't broken her body physically that night, though God knows she had plenty of bruises and sprains and dislocated fingers and even one shoulder. All that was truly damaged was her trust and her heart and, of course, her soul. She'd come to understand the healing effect of the animals because she'd spent more time downstairs with them than she had upstairs in her own medical bed. She had needed that. Later she'd emerged feeling a whole lot more balanced. Capable of smiling again, even though she still didn't talk about it. Her father had brought it up once or twice but only as a sign that she was handling life better now.

How interesting that he hadn't said anything about Aaron. Because, yes, Aaron was dealing with some difficult stuff, but she didn't see the same issues of abuse inherent in him—despite his own father being abusive. After all, Levi wasn't like that. Maybe she should ask her father, just for added confirmation. If she had listened to his advice about Jim in the first place, things wouldn't have gotten so bad.

As she walked into the house, she found her father sitting in front of the big picture window overlooking the complex, holding a cup of tea. She walked over and sat down, slipping her hand into his free one.

He looked at her for a long moment and then said, "You've been looking very happy these last few days. What's bothering you now?"

"Earlier you said Aaron would have a hard time adapting." She searched his eyes. "Did you mean he would end up like Jim?"

He placed his cup of tea down, his eyebrows shooting upward. "Oh, my dear, no. No, not at all. I don't see the same abuse or violence in Aaron. Believe me, if you were falling down that rabbit hole again, I would have said so immediately. No. That's not it. What I do see is self-incrimination. He blames himself for something terrible. Like he's a prisoner to this issue. He has to let it go, or he'll never be happy. And, by extension, you won't be either."

She reached her arms around her dad and hugged him tight. "I thought about Gram today," Dani said as she settled in her chair next to Dad. "I miss her."

Her father smiled. "She was a force, that's for sure."

"I'm grateful she helped raise me," Dani said. "I'm even

more grateful she was there when you were sick. Because I didn't know who else to turn to. Without her, I would have been lost."

"You and me both," he admitted. "In my darkest days, she swung the light so I could find the way back. I knew, deep down, that I needed to be there for you, but she had to point that out to me." He shook his head. "She never let me forget it was my duty to make the best of every day and to not just walk away because it was easy." He laughed. "Sometimes nothing was easy about my life, but you? Well, you are truly a blessing."

He grabbed her hand again. "This is the happiest time of my life now. You have put so much life and energy into this place," he said. "To see all of it coming together, and to have all these new friends coming to this place, then going on to have full and satisfied lives ... Well, you should be happy with what you've accomplished."

She smiled and shook her head. "This isn't what *I* accomplished, Dad. It's what *we* accomplished."

They sat in companionable silence for a while, looking out the window as the sun slowly settled over top of the complex. Just when she thought she might get up and make herself a cup of tea, he asked in a low voice, "What will you do when it's time for him to leave?"

She settled back into place. "What do you mean?"

He turned to look at her directly. His gaze was clear and honest but also searching as he studied her. "His life isn't here. He'll leave and pick up the pieces of wherever his life was. Will you stay, or will you leave?"

She stared at him in astonishment. "I'm not leaving. I'm not going anywhere."

"Aren't you?" he asked quietly, sadly. "What if it's the

only way you can keep Aaron?"

She stared at him in stunned amazement. It had never even occurred to her, but it was possible Aaron would need to leave. If that happened, what would she do? Her voice low, she gave her dad the truth. "I have no idea."

AARON LEANED AGAINST the fence, watching her as she walked toward her house, her trim figure moving smartly. She stopped to caress one of the horses, who nickered at her across the fence. He smiled. She did love animals.

The center was an ideal place for her. This was where she belonged.

As soon as that thought crossed his mind, he shuffled around so he could stare out across the fence and horses. If this was where she belonged, it followed that she wouldn't be happy if she had to leave. Could she leave? This was her place. Not like she could just sell her shares and move on. Although she could hire a new manager fairly easily. But she and her father had fashioned this place into what it was today.

So what about him then? Was he thinking about a permanent relationship with her?

No doubt that he wanted more, but he was hardly a good bet. He didn't have a job. He was settling into his physio and scheduled for a minor surgery here. Martha, one of the team, had intimated that after a couple tweaks on the stump, he could have a different—better—prosthesis made. In other words, he was healing. He looked forward to a future that wouldn't require him to stay here. But if he wasn't here, then how would he carry on a relationship with

Dani? If he wanted to further that relationship, how did he stay here?

He stared out across at the pasture, tormented by the unending thoughts. His surroundings were truly stunning, but what did he have to contribute? He was a soldier. A fighting machine. Or, at least, that was what he had been. He didn't have very many skills that he could convert to a civilian life. He understood he was at a crossroads and capable of making his own choices right now.

Stan had said he could use the help, but that didn't mean the center could afford to hire somebody. It was one thing for Aaron to stay here and help out while he was a patient, but it was an entirely different matter to help out afterward but not get paid. That obviously wouldn't work either. How could he live with himself if his wife supported him? He was all for women's rights, sure, but that "kept man" scenario wouldn't work for him either. He needed to at least help financially in a relationship and be a fully independent, contributing member of society. He didn't care about who was the so-called breadwinner of the family, but he needed to know that, should anything happen and the center be forced to close down, he was fully capable of supporting her.

Just thinking about the word "wife" made him feel warm inside. Was it even possible? With a final glance at the fields, he realized no answers were out there, so he grabbed his crutches and slowly made his way back to his room.

He hoped his brother would call soon. He opened his wallet and pulled out the only picture he had of Levi. After a decade of hoping to never hear his brother's voice again, all he could do now was wait and stare at the phone, wishing that something would finally break for him.

He sat down on the bed, only mildly tired. He was getting stronger. All because he was here.

The center had a hell of a system. How he'd gotten in, he didn't know. With his upcoming surgery and the cost of the prosthesis ... The military had covered him for months, but then he'd been informed he was now down to his disability pension. Just what did that mean? Seemed to him the permanent loss of his leg—not to mention the end of his military career—entitled him to some permanent benefits. He would make the needed phone calls tomorrow to see where he stood. After that, he could plan. Maybe he would go back to school. He'd saved for years, but would it be enough?

Then again, maybe there was no money for such dreams. He didn't know if any navy benefits would allow him to rehabilitate himself into a new career—or if grant money was available for him. But it was certainly worth asking, and for the first time, he realized he would ask. He'd let life run its own course for a long time. Now he would pick up the reins and direct the way he wanted to go.

Soon he was in bed, pleased and happy to see that his body was not totally exhausted this time. When his phone rang, he checked the caller ID. *His brother.* Excited, yet nervous at the same time, he pushed himself into a sitting position and answered.

"Aaron, it's Levi."

Levi's tone was grim, and Aaron's heart sank. "I gather there's no news?"

"There is news," Levi said cautiously. "Your MIA buddy might not be MIA. We've got word he's in Afghanistan, operating as a mercenary."

Aaron straightened. "You ran him down?"

"Not yet," Levi cautioned. "But the intel seems good. We've spoken to a friend in Africa who has contacts there. With any luck, we can talk to him."

"Even if you do, no way he'll tell you the truth. It's not his style." Aaron knew that fact, to his own detriment.

"Yeah, but we're hoping somebody will talk to him and gain his trust."

Aaron was silent, thinking about Levi's suggestion.

Then Levi added, "This issue could take a little bit longer to resolve than we'd hoped."

"And therefore costly," Aaron said flatly. "I don't have any money to help pay for this."

"I didn't ask for any money," Levi snapped. "Just pulling in a few favors. No money's exchanging hands here at all."

Aaron took a deep breath. "Good to know," he said in a more neutral tone. "I'm a little sensitive on that whole charity thing."

An odd silence hovered on the other end, but then his brother didn't know him anymore either. Had they ever known each other?

Levi remained silent, so Aaron continued. "Thanks for the update. Let me know if you track him down in person. Even proving he's alive would be a big help. The navy didn't believe me when I said Cain had walked away. If they catch him, that proves one of my statements, and maybe that will give credence to the others as well."

"Will do."

Aaron stared down at the phone in his hand, excitement surging through his system. It would be hard to sleep now because not just excitement bothered him—there was anger too. To think that asshole had created a whole new life for himself, with no repercussions for his actions, was untenable.

No way could Aaron let that continue, but without proof, he couldn't move forward.

No money had changed hands. Good. He didn't want to be beholden to Levi in any way. He didn't want to owe anybody and definitely not his brother. It just went back to that whole sibling rivalry thing, having an older brother looking after him. At this point, he wanted to be his own man. Hell, he already was his own man. He didn't need his brother's charity.

He didn't need charity from anyone.

Except that small voice in the back of his head told him he *was* already accepting his brother's help. That finding Cain was charity on Levi's part. But Aaron had damned-well accepted it as his only option. Yet, he also recognized how it was very good of Levi to even consider this.

Then he understood. If somebody had treated Levi that way, Aaron would have stepped up too.

Reminding him, blood *was* thicker than water.

Chapter 13

T HE NEXT MORNING, Dani stood in the doorway of Aaron's bedroom. She found it empty, even though it was earlier than normal. Frowning, she went to the reception area and on through to the dining room, built around a big circular layout. No matter which direction she took, she would end up in the big open space where breakfast was being served. She studied everybody seated at the tables but still saw no sign of him. Trying to appear casual, she poured herself a cup of coffee and wandered onto the deck, searching. Maybe he'd gone out with the animals. She'd done that a few times, particularly after a bad night. The animals offered comfort that few humans could because along with that comfort, they didn't add judgment. What a glorious feeling to know they accepted you and didn't care about the other issues in your life.

She took the stairs down to the lower level and heard a splash in the pool. Then she knew. He'd gone for an early morning swim. With a bright smile on her face, she walked to the edge of the pool and studied him. He'd either had a hell of a bad night or had woken up to a hell of a bad morning because he wasn't just swimming, he was driving his body forward, forcing it to be stronger. She'd never seen him swim this hard or this fast. A relentless determination was in his strokes, as if he could outswim something bothering him.

When he flipped and turned at the far end and came back and then repeated it again and again and again, she knew something was seriously wrong. With her heart sinking, she sat down casually to wait. When he finally broke off and stopped, his lungs were heaving, and he gasped for air. She waited for him to turn and look around, only he didn't. He rolled onto his back and did a lazy backstroke to the shallow end. There he pulled himself up and sat on the side of the pool.

"Good morning," she said in a low voice.

He turned to look at her, but no smile was on his face. From the fatigue in his muscles, it looked like he'd overdone the swimming too.

"That was quite a swim you just had," she said in a neutral tone.

He shook his head. "I don't know about a swim, but it felt like the devil was chasing me." He grabbed his towel and quickly ran it over his face and his upper body. He maneuvered to the bench and pulled himself up. There, he strapped on one of the early prosthetic prototypes, with extra padding around his stump, and grabbed his crutches, just in case. He slowly made his way to her.

As he grew closer, she saw his hands trembling. She quickly got up and pulled out a chair for him. "Sit down," she scolded. "You've overdone it again."

He shook his head. "Did I?" He gave her a lopsided grin and said, "It's probably a good thing. Tough night. I needed to work off some frustration."

She slowly retook her chair. "What brought it on?"

"Levi called me." He studied the coffee cup in her hand and then looked at the stairs, as if contemplating whether he had the energy to make the trip.

She kept her gaze on his, her heart tingling in worry at the thought of what Levi might've said. "And?"

Aaron shrugged. "Some intel came back saying the asshole who did this to me may be working as a mercenary in Afghanistan."

Her mouth dropped open, and she stared at him. "Oh, my God, that's wonderful news!"

He stared at her moodily. "Is it? So he has gone on to live the life he wanted, with no repercussions for his actions, and yet look at the end result for me ..." He pointed to where his leg should be.

She reached across and covered his fingers with hers. "It also means that, if anybody can catch him, they can prove he isn't MIA and that you didn't lie."

"That's what I told Levi. But it still doesn't mean Cain will admit to what he did. Because, of course, why would he? He killed two US soldiers."

She gently stroked his hand, trying to find the right words to help him deal with this. She now understood the drive behind the swimming. Maybe it'd been the best thing for him after all, but he'd obviously overdone it because he was shaky and exhausted. "Do you want a cup of coffee?" she asked.

He shook his head. "No more making it easy on me. If I want coffee, I'll get up the damned stairs and get coffee. Bad enough Levi's doing this instead of me handling it."

"You have a real problem with charity, don't you?" she asked quietly, her heart sinking. If he had any idea what she and Levi had concocted between them to get Aaron here ... She finally understood just how big a problem that would be for him.

He stared at her, silent.

"Maybe you should change your perspective on that and see it as a helping hand," she pressed on. "If people don't know you're in need, they can't help. Sometimes they have to be told."

"I don't want to accept a helping hand."

"Nobody wants to be in a position where they have to accept a helping hand," she retorted. "But you, my father and even I have all done it when necessary. So you accept it. You get back on your feet, and then you move forward. If you can pay it back, you do, and if not, you accept that you will turn around and help somebody else when the time is right." By now her voice had turned hard and snappy.

She liked a lot of things about Aaron but not his "poor me" attitude. He would have to get over that damned fast because she wouldn't take much more of it. She also knew fear was driving her because once Aaron found out about Levi paying for his brother's stay here, the shit would hit the fan. And she'd be part of the fallout. If that was the case, she would do all she could to push this guy, mentally, physically and emotionally. Then he could move on to have a good life. Even if that meant without her.

But instead of her words spurring him into action, he studied her, his brows knit together on his forehead. She realized she'd opened a can of worms she hadn't meant to.

"You never mentioned you were here in a hospital bed."

She sat back and gave him a cool stare. "Why should I?"

At that he had the grace to blush. "I'm sorry. That's your private matter. And I'm being a bit of a bear, aren't I?"

She gave a serious and decisive nod. "Yes. Lots of people are here to help you, but they can only help you if you're willing to accept it. There's not always a price tag for help in this world."

She picked up her cup, finished it and said, "I'm getting a second cup of coffee." With that she turned and walked up the stairs. She didn't look to see if he was following her. If he didn't want any more help, that was fine with her. She wouldn't deliver any more cups of tea or coffee, even though she had no problem with that. Because to her, that wasn't charity. It was being kind. Being nice. She understood he hadn't had a whole lot of that in his life. But that was no excuse. It was time he learned.

"SHIT." HE STARED at Dani's retreating back as she took the stairs. He'd certainly pissed her off and only now realized how he had offended her about helping people. That was what she did at the center. Here he had this opportunity, and instead of appreciating what he had, he was getting his back up at the thought of the least bit of charity. Like when she'd bring him a cup of coffee. Which was often. Since when had that become a charity thing? He felt like a heel. At the same time, some residual anger about Cain still ran through him. He'd also overdone it in the pool, and he knew therapy would be a bitch today.

But it wasn't—it was much worse.

As if understanding how emotionally messed up he was today, the physiotherapist focused those negative energies of Aaron's into working on his back with some weight-lifting exercises. There'd been such strong promise lately as Aaron could feel his strength building up, slowly but surely. The pain had even eased, but right now, Shane was all about getting down to the meat and working those muscles hard.

Then the physiotherapist said something magical.

"If you keep up progress like this, you may not need that surgery at all."

Aaron turned to stare at Shane. "It's a possibility?" He would do anything to avoid that surgery.

"We weren't sure you'd need the fifth surgery when you got here, and now that your muscles are strengthening and building up, there's a good chance we can fix this without more invasive cutting and stitching," he said.

Aaron bowed his head for a moment, giving silent thanks for this.

Then he went at it hard again.

If he had any hope of getting back to where he was before—strong, agile and fit for duty—even though, with the missing leg, the military would never accept him now, he would still do his damnedest.

He wouldn't fail because of a lack of effort.

When the session was done, he stood, wavering on his foot, sweat dripping off his face, goose bumps popping up all over from the supreme sense of power rippling through him.

"Massage time. You need a heavy, deep one today."

"I do. I can feel the muscles trying to knot."

"Well, we're not letting them. Let's go."

They moved over to the table where Aaron took off his shirt and wiped the sweat from his body. The window was open, letting in a cool breeze. The therapist had left, and Aaron knew Chuck would be in soon. He was a hell of a masseur, and he and Shane took turns at the different shifts.

Stripping down to his boxers, he rolled over and let his body flop on the long bench. Even that hurt like shit. He had overdone it.

But if it got him back to health—without more surgeries—then it was all worth it.

Chuck came in a few minutes later and worked Aaron's muscles deeply, kneading to release the tension and knots. The worst massage session ever. By the time Chuck was done, Aaron wanted to cry with relief.

"Sauna, then shower. Let those muscles rest. We'll skip this afternoon's physio."

Chuck walked to the door and then turned back. "Next time you need to work off some frustration, ease up before you trash yourself. We can't have you slowing your progress with an injury."

Injury. Odd, Aaron hadn't even considered that. If a pulled muscle could easily sideline him, or much worse, if that muscle was in his back ...

For the first time he understood how stupid his frantic swimming session this morning had been. He'd wanted to release that building rage, but he hadn't thought it out.

As someone ... maybe Dani ... had said, it was all about balance.

Chapter 14

GOOD THING SHE had a ton of work to keep the niggle of fear and resentment at bay. She knew how detrimental negative thinking was. The rules were no different for herself than anyone else here.

"Dani?"

She looked up to see Stan in the doorway, a hesitant smile on his face.

"What's up?"

"I wondered … if you have a moment, could we talk?"

"Sure." She waved at the chair opposite her desk.

He closed the door. "I know there are programs for those who don't have enough money to come here, and you tap into those all the time, but do you know of any for retraining some of the men?"

She frowned, her mind running across the various programs. "A lot of grant money is available, but each has a set of criteria to be met in order to apply. If they are veterans, some money is there, but they'd have to go through their own channels for that."

"Right." He looked out the window. "I was thinking about Aaron."

"Oh," she said in surprise. "Is this something he's been talking to you about?"

"He always planned to go to vet school, but after his

mother died, he ended up in the military. Vet school would be four more years."

"He is a veteran, so money could very well be there for him to achieve those goals," she said. "But it's not that easy to get into the program, is it?"

"He does need references and preferably some work experience, but no reason he can't do it." Stan shrugged. "He's a young man, and this would give him a wonderful future, particularly as it was his original passion."

"What is it you want me to do?"

Stan stared at her. "I can see this relationship developing between you two. Has he mentioned anything about his future?"

"Not really." She shook her head again. "I don't think he can see that far ahead yet. He's waiting on a bigger issue to be resolved first. In a way he's completely blocked until it is."

"Oh."

"And again why?"

"Well, I offered him some hands-on experience helping me here. And, since I'm on the board, I wondered about writing a recommendation for him."

She raised her eyebrows. "It would be a nice thing for you to do, but maybe you should ask him about it first. Because if it's something he's only considering but isn't serious about, then there's no point putting in the effort."

Stan stood and said, "I was hoping you'd bring it up with him and see what he says. Because what he tells me might be something different than what he tells you."

She considered that. People often did just as Stan had described. Sometimes they were just making conversation and didn't understand how somebody else perceived their words. She nodded. "Okay, I can do that."

Stan's expression became one of relief. "Thanks. Of course I can't guarantee he'll get in. But if you would agree to let him do volunteer work here, then it would help his chances. Like you said, there are ways to make it happen, but I don't want to be pushing myself in where I am not wanted."

She agreed with that part. The only person who could answer these questions was Aaron himself. It wasn't a light undertaking to go to veterinary school, involving years of dedicated hard work and effort. So it had to be something he hadn't just casually tossed up in haste. He needed to commit himself to a major undertaking. She agreed with Stan in the sense that, if Aaron wanted this, there were ways and means to make it happen.

Of course she also had to pick the right time to discuss it with him. She wasn't sure that was right now. She knew today was a positive step forward after hearing Levi's news, but she could understand how it would bring up a ton of negative emotions for Aaron. She stared down at her coffee cup and wondered if she should check in on him. It was almost four o'clock.

He'd had a long hard day already. She picked up her coffee cup. His room was in one of the short side hallways, so she couldn't casually walk past. She headed straight there but found the door shut. She frowned and checked the schedule on the door, but he didn't have anything noted for right now. It also didn't mean he was inside. She knocked once, then twice. No answer. She turned and headed back to her office. He might be sleeping, or he could be visiting with others. No way to know. However, if she wanted to track him down, she knew of one very likely place to find him.

She caught sight of Shane at the front desk, talking to

one of the new girls.

A lot of the staff members were single, and bringing in just one new person always caused a shift in the energy of the place. So far Melissa seemed to be working out fine. She'd been to hell and back herself because of a car accident, so she certainly understood what rehab entailed and could empathize with everybody in the center. To date her sympathy had seemed genuine, as well as her interest in everyone's well-being. As long as she was capable of doing the job, Dani couldn't ask much more of anyone.

Shane noticed Dani and headed in her direction. "Hey, Dani. How's it going?"

She leaned against the doorjamb of her office and smiled at the man who'd worked for them for five years now. He was very popular with the patients, considered a hard taskmaster but fair, which was a great balance for the residents. "Not too bad. Aaron really knocked himself out in the pool."

"He sure did. Physio was pretty rough on him afterward too. I believe he's sleeping right now." He shook his head. "I suggested speaking with his counselors before next week, so he could work through some issues. Obviously something prompted the hard swim this morning."

"That was a good suggestion. Hopefully he'll take you up on it." She doubted it, but she was willing to give Aaron a chance to prove her wrong. He couldn't stay stubborn all his life.

Just most of it.

Considering his day, and not having touched base with him earlier, she hung around the office a little later than normal, then walked through the common room to see if he'd shown up yet. When she saw no sign of him, she headed for the dinner buffet and studied the patrons. It was early yet, so not too many were eating, but the ones who were appeared to be enjoying it. She walked along the buffet, just to see just what was on offer. She found it hard to resist the fragrant baked ham and roast beef right at the end. Maybe she'd eat here after all. She smiled up at the chef. "This looks awesome, Gabriel."

He smiled back. "Grab a plate and sit down and enjoy. You work too hard."

She laughed and shook her head. "Why do you keep telling me that?"

"You know it's true." He didn't give her much choice. He lifted a plate from the stack and served her a slice of ham and a slice of roast beef. He nudged her down the aisle. "The broccoli in cheese sauce just came out of the oven. It's good."

It was hard to refuse at that point, so she helped herself to a serving of the vegetables and sat down on the deck. She was hungry, having foregone lunch. She had to get out of the habit of missing meals. No food, just work wasn't how it was supposed to be. As she enjoyed her meal, a shadow fell across the table. She looked up to see Aaron.

"Do you mind if I sit?" His voice was gruff.

Before she had a chance to answer, he sat down—heavily. She looked at him in concern. "Are you sure you shouldn't go back to bed?"

He raised his head and glanced her way. "I'll be fine," he muttered. "I need to eat so my muscles can heal."

Definitely a day where he had done too much. Even his voice was heavy and tired. His face had no color, and his lips looked bloodless. Alarmed, she said, "Part of me wants to get the doctor."

She was already out of her chair when he stopped her.

"No doctor. I'm fine. Just tired. I wouldn't object to a cup of coffee though, if you don't mind."

She poured him a cup, at the same time snagging a small plate and picking up two cream puffs. Depending on where his blood sugar was, these would help him. She brought his snack and drink to him, relieved to see he looked a little better now that he was resting. Obviously the trip from his room to her had been enough to wear him down. That wasn't good. She'd hoped he'd made better progress than that by now.

She placed the cup and plate in front of him and sat down to finish her food. "I guess you won't be going for another crazy swim again anytime soon."

"No," he said. "This'll set me back a few days."

"Only a few days? Good," she said with a bright smile. "Nothing you can't recover from, and now you better know your limits."

He looked at her for a long moment and then smiled. "You're always optimistic. You see sunshine and roses instead of the reality."

"It's only your reality if you let it be," she replied calmly. "I prefer—no, I choose to—see the bright side. There is enough negativity in my world. I don't need any more."

He devoured the two cream puffs and then slowly sipped his coffee as he watched her eat. "Dinner looks good."

She nodded, her mouth stuffed with broccoli. He glanced over at the buffet table. She could see him contemplating getting there on his own. She swallowed and said, "Give me a minute, and I'll get a plate for you." She watched his mouth open to protest. In a low, hard voice, she said, "Remember, there is a time to accept help."

He stared at her and then slumped in his chair, resting.

"Thank you. I think I will accept your kind offer."

She laughed. "That was hard for you, wasn't it?"

"Damned right it was." But he had a big grin on his face.

HE WATCHED HER leave. She was just so damned nice, he felt like he had no business being beside her. She was so clean and fresh and honest, and he felt dirty. This stain on his soul—would it ever get clean? Levi and his people were doing their best to track down the man responsible. As a last resort, they might end up forcefully capturing Cain. As far as Aaron was concerned, they could kill the bastard, but Aaron wanted Cain to come clean first, and Aaron wanted the proof to go to the brass upstairs.

For all he knew, the brass had changed. Very likely the people who thought Aaron had lied weren't even around anymore. He stared down at his clenched fists. So close and yet so far away. It was all out of his hands. That was what got to him. He could do nothing to make this any better. He couldn't grab his old buddy and pound the truth out of him. As far as Aaron knew, his brother was probably the best person for the job, but what if even he failed?

How helpless would Aaron feel then?

Yet, he couldn't have asked more of his brother. Still, the waiting, sitting and more waiting were killing Aaron, even though he had a wonderful place to do it in—a supportive and strong place, helping him get better day by day. However, in his anger, he had set back his progress. His ire was to be expected, after getting the news he had. Even now, the tension still ran through his muscles, even after swimming too hard, lifting weights too heavy. Aaron knew better—

now—to push his body further.

His brother was doing what he could. All Aaron could do was sit back and wait.

No, he needed to do what he could do – and that was heal. The truth, while it would set part of him free, getting healthy, strong and fit again, well, that would offer him a whole new future.

Chapter 15

D ANI WOKE UP to birds singing and sunshine floating into her bedroom. She bounced out of bed, had a quick shower and dressed, then raced to the center. She was eager to see Aaron, but then this had been her routine for weeks.

She hurried through the center, waving happily and calling out morning greetings to everyone in her path. She stopped at her office to confirm she had no emergency messages, and then she carried on to Aaron's room. It was empty, but then that was no surprise. He'd been steadily gaining in strength and doing a lot more every day. She grabbed a cup of coffee and walked onto the deck. "Good morning, George. Have you seen Aaron?"

George smiled at her and said, "Last I saw him, he was with your father, and things were looking pretty serious." He shrugged his shoulders and said, "Aaron didn't look upset or anything. Just looked like he wanted answers."

"Answers?" she repeated back.

But George had no further information. She looked around but found no sign of either man. Feeling slightly worried, she wandered down to the pool level, searching for them. No sign. She walked through the doors and found the two of them sitting at one of the poker tables where her dad played a lot.

The conversation did not look good.

With a sinking heart, she probably understood exactly what was going on. She walked straight over and placed her cup down and sat. "Good morning," she said with a forced cheerfulness. "I've been looking all over for you."

Silence reigned.

She studied her father's face, but he wouldn't look her in the eye. She turned her gaze toward Aaron and found him glaring at her. She raised her eyebrows. "What's the matter, Aaron?" She kept her tone pleasant but cool.

"Why didn't you tell me?"

"Tell you what?" She frowned, not willing to confirm anything—yet.

"That I'm a charity case here?"

"No one is a charity case here," she replied, adding a bite to her tone. "That just insults everyone."

Aaron's glare deepened. "Who is paying for my care here?"

"A donor, who asked to remain anonymous." She crossed her arms over her chest and glared back at him. "You might want to consider that you're one of the lucky ones."

"Or you might want to consider I won't like what's going on here," he shot back. "If not, why didn't you say something about it at the beginning?"

"*Because* the donor asked to remain anonymous," she repeated. "*Because* we didn't want anything to slow down your healing." She leaned forward, into his personal space. "*And* you might want to consider that you've come a hell of a long way very quickly. Where else have you had such success?" She paused, giving him ample time to reply.

He settled back against his chair, looking like he wanted to say something.

She sat and waited. Inside, her heart was breaking, but she was resolute. Donors were an important part of this project, and she couldn't have him getting on his high horse just because somebody had offered to help before he was ready to accept it. "We ensured that *nothing* slowed your progress down."

"You lied to me."

She gasped. "I did not."

"Yes, you did. If not in actual fact, then in concept." He sneered. "Is that the only way you can get a man? Pick one who's not quite whole and have him see you as a savior? Well, I don't need a helping hand from anyone. Especially not you." He stood up and hobbled shakily out of the room.

Dani sat there, her breath shaky, as she watched him exit.

Her father reached across the table and grabbed her hand. "Give him a chance to get over it," he said in a soothing voice.

She shook her head. In her mind, he was an idiot not to see the great advantage he'd been given. If there was one thing she hated, it was a lack of appreciation for receiving donor money. She could deal with not being appreciated herself, but she sure as hell thought Aaron should appreciate the rare gift he'd been given. "There shouldn't be anything to get over. It's his damned pride and ego. He needs to take a step back and let that go."

"Whoa there, Nellie," her father said in a reasonable tone. "I know you can understand when a man is down as low as Aaron was, the only thing he has is his pride. His ego keeps him propped up. Inflate that ego a little more, and he can face the world with a big smirk and an 'I don't give a shit' attitude. But if you take that away ..." He patted her hand and nodded to himself. "Just give him some time. Wait for this to all blow over, and he'll be fine."

She doubted it, but even if he did get over it, would she? It didn't matter. Nothing else could be said at the moment. She deliberately turned the conversation to different things until she finished her coffee. Then she stood, dropping a kiss on his forehead. "Thanks for always being here, Dad."

"I didn't want to be here this morning, to tell you the truth. But he cornered me."

She gave him a big hug. "He had no right to do that, but as we know, he's not been thinking things through lately."

She picked up both of their empty cups and returned to the dining area. She placed the cups on one of the trays for dirty dishes and headed to her office. Her relationship with Aaron had shifted and would never revert back. *He'll leave now.* She stood at the window and stared out at the horses. *This is where I need to be regardless.* No way would she tell Aaron who his benefactor was because it would just make him angrier.

In her continued desire to help him, she had found herself caught between a rock and a hard place. The principles of the center were very clear. When a donor asked to remain anonymous, she did just that. She wouldn't violate such a request. Since the funds came from a friend of hers, she was doubly invested to keep his secret. Which would make it just that much worse from Aaron's viewpoint.

Levi had called her, thinking her place could help Aaron. She had agreed. She wanted to help. Levi had offered to pay outright, even though she had explained their four-patient policy for pro bono treatment. She'd transferred Aaron here to offer him the best of the center's abilities, and yes, she'd been curious. Once upon a time, Aaron had been such a driving force in her life that she'd wanted to see him again. But that was not how business decisions were made here. So, at Levi's request, she'd put his brother's file before the team for approval. They had all gone over Aaron's history and each had given the go-ahead. The team had said yes, and they had the needed funds. All Aaron had to do was get better.

He had done that in spades. She just didn't know what he would do now.

How stupid she was to get involved with anybody at the center. She buried herself in work for a few hours, until a knock came at the door, and she looked up to see Dr. Herzog. She smiled at him, but he didn't smile back. She leaned back and crossed her arms. "What's the problem?"

He took a hesitant step inside the door and said, "Aaron Hammond requested a transfer out."

Dani stilled the knots in her stomach, even though she had expected this. It came as a shock regardless.

"Did he give a reason?" She hoped he'd kept their relationship out of it because she still had to work with everybody in a professional capacity, and it would be damned hard to do if they thought she was the reason behind a patient's transfer.

"Something about not being anybody's charity case ..." Dr. Herzog's voice trailed off. "I asked him to explain, but he went silent." He came farther into the room and sat in the guest chair. "He's done really well. We've been thoroughly impressed with his dedication to his own healing. Whatever's going on right now, it's not good. It's better if he stays here for at least another month, but if he wants to go, we can't stop him."

She nodded. "Do you think it'd do any good if I talked

to him?"

"He asked specifically that nobody talk him out of it."

She pulled a pad of paper toward her. "Where does he want to go?"

The doctor stood up, relief evident in his voice. "I don't think he has any idea. Maybe you can make a few phone calls and find a place for him?"

She nodded. "I can give him the general contact information for the VA office. Once he's settled where he wants to be, they can tell him which VA hospital would be nearest to him."

Dr. Herzog nodded back. "I guess that's the only option he has."

"His problem is somebody generously donated for his care. Yet, he got his back up when he found out." She shrugged. "It's his option to return to the VA hospital. His choice."

After the doctor left, she sat there, frozen for a moment, figuring out what her own options were. She still couldn't tell Aaron about Levi being the donor. And it no longer mattered because Aaron was leaving anyway. However, she could do one last thing. She reached for the phone. When a woman's voice answered, she said, "Ice, is Levi there? I need to talk to him about his brother."

Levi came on the phone. "Dani? What's up?"

She tried to explain, but when grief overtook her, she began to sob.

"I'll be there in the morning," was all Levi said.

She hung up the phone and wiped away the tears. She needed to get out of here. She needed to go someplace where her love and affection would be accepted and not rejected. The animals. She stopped in little Molly's stall, delighted to see her now snuggling up against Maggie. The two enjoyed seeing her. She spent several minutes cuddling them both and then walked out and did the rounds. Enough animals were here that any time she needed to mend her broken heart, they came willingly. How sad that she was likely to be here every day for a while now.

Still, she'd been in this position before. This was nothing new. She would overcome it like she had everything else. Feeling a tiny bit better, she walked home. Tonight she just wanted to be alone.

ANGER STILL BURNED through Aaron. He pushed himself harder and felt heavier than he ever had before. Every one of his team told him to ease back and take it easy, but he just couldn't. It burned him to think he wasn't here just because his VA benefits covered it. The knowledge that he was here because some unnamed person had paid his bill churned in his gut. A charity case! He was damn sure nobody's charity case. He had money. Maybe not enough money for this, but he had money to go to a decent center. Sure, he'd received great care here, and he'd enjoyed his time, but that didn't mean he couldn't get the same care somewhere else. That was what his VA benefits were for, right?

Nobody needed to pay for him. He'd always been capable of looking after himself. Even when he got to his room last night, he hadn't been able to resist doing sit-ups and push-ups. Now it was morning, and he had essentially had no rest. His stomach churned, his head was heavy, and he kept feeding it with more anger. Because the only thing he had left was anger. Betrayal was something he'd lived with for so long that, sure, maybe he was looking for it in other people, but ... he hadn't expected to find it anymore. Not really.

He'd thought she was different.

But just like his best friend who had blown him to shit over in Afghanistan, she'd blown him to shit here on home soil. He couldn't accept that.

A hard knock came at the door. He considered ignoring it, when it came again. The forceful knock made him realize he couldn't evade the upcoming confrontation. That was just fine with him as he was spoiling for a fight. If anybody from the center tried to stop him, well, they could get the hell out of his way as he was leaving as soon as he could. Today if possible.

"Come in," he snapped, ready to stand up to whatever was coming.

The door slammed open, and Levi stepped inside—a very cold and angry Levi.

The surprise at seeing his brother pushed Aaron back to the bed. Suddenly, he was afraid this had something to do with the favor Levi was doing for him. "What's the matter?"

Levi turned and slammed the door shut, before confronting his brother. "You're the problem."

"What?" Aaron frowned at him, anger churning in his gut again. The temper that hadn't been very far under the surface since yesterday was firing already. "What are you talking about?"

In typical Levi fashion, he didn't hold back. "How dare you target Dani for your little pricked ego. I'm the one who hooked you up with her center after the grapevine told me about your tirade at Walter Reed, needing 'a change of scenery.'" He took a breath. "I knew how much progress the patients here were making. So I'm the one who paid for your care here. I'm the one who asked Dani to not tell you. You have a problem with that, then you tell me." He took three steps closer to his brother and glared at him. "I'm right here. You want to take a swing at me? Do it. Get it out of your system. But it'll be a long, cold day in hell before I let you blame Dani for something you should be thanking her for, and on your knees while doing it. So stop acting like a pissed-off child, throwing a temper tantrum."

Aaron's jaw dropped. He shook his head. "Why? Why tell Dani not to tell me?"

"If you'd known I had paid for it, would you still have come?"

"No. Hell, no."

"Which is exactly why I told Dani not to tell you."

He stared at his brother. Five minutes ago, he thought nothing could have taken the temper right out of him, but Levi had shoved a fist down Aaron's throat, grabbing that fiery red ball of emotion and tossing it right out the window. Aaron sagged on the bed. He instantly realized what he had done to Dani. He'd blamed her for something she had no choice in. Because, just like Levi, when she made a promise, she kept it.

"I didn't want to be a charity case," Aaron muttered. "All I could think about was that I was no longer a man, no longer capable of standing on my own two feet, doing what needed to be done. Here people had to pitch in to treat me, bolster me so I could do what needed to be done."

"Don't be stupid. We all need help sometimes." Levi glared at his brother. "You think I liked staying in the hospital for so long? Do you think I'd have stayed if I wasn't forced to?" Levi shook his head and paced back and forth.

"Do you think Dani didn't have other people lined up to come here? Even now she has dozens of people to take your place." He leaned forward and shoved his face into Aaron's. "She did this as a favor to me. So you owe her a goddamned apology. If you don't want to be here one more day, that's fine with all of us. You pick where you want to live and transfer to whatever VA hospital you can get into. Then you can get the hell out of here." Levi waved his hand dismissively at him. "You're damned near well anyway. You could go home and look after yourself from here on out."

He turned around, slammed the door open one last time, and walked out, not even bothering to slam it closed.

Aaron was left with the shambles of the mess he'd brought on.

He stared at the empty doorway, realizing Levi would likely have gone straight to Dani. Just where Aaron should've gone first when he had questions. When he had doubts. He should've trusted that she was doing what she needed to do. Instead, he got on his high horse and ripped into her, and for that, Levi was not very happy. It was a stupid thing to do. Of course, it had taken his older brother to show him the way.

Feeling like the little boy he'd been accused of being, he slowly made his way to Dani's office, only to find it empty. He took a deep breath and realized that if he had to apologize publicly that was a punishment he well deserved. He made his way to the main buffet area and saw both Levi and Dani sitting on the deck outside in the sun. Levi was holding Dani's hands in his. It was a jolt. Nothing could've made Aaron feel more like a heel than seeing his brother comfort the woman who Aaron loved. He felt like such an asshole.

He approached them quietly. Levi looked up and glared at him. When Dani saw Levi's face, she stiffened. Aaron knew he wasn't exactly welcome. He ignored that and stepped forward.

"I'm sorry, Dani. I had no right to blame you or to push you into telling me who my donor was. But to me, it was yet another betrayal. I didn't think I could handle that again. Not from you. So Levi brought the truth home to me this visit. I am sorry." He took a deep breath. "I don't need any more physio or medical treatments that I can't get locally. I'll pack my bags and leave today."

He turned and walked away, but she interrupted him. "How could you think you're the only one dealing with betrayal?" Her voice was low and hard, but he could hear the pain in it. She pointed at Levi. "You know your own brother's story."

She stood and faced Aaron. "Now here's mine. My last relationship ripped me apart physically and mentally, but I put myself back together, and I recovered. *Here.* In a hospital bed. Just like you. But what you said to me ripped me apart emotionally, down to my very soul. I'll take a lot longer to heal from that. Betrayal is *not* a two-way street. Just because you were betrayed doesn't give you the right to treat others the same way." She glared at him. "This center is where we give to each other. Where we accept that we *all* need help. It's a place where we're free and comfortable to both give and receive charity. There is no debt. There are no checks and balances here. We're all here for one thing, and that is to help people move forward," she snapped. "The problem with you is *you.*"

Spinning on her heel, she turned her back on him and stalked away.

Aaron turned to look at his brother, but Levi was already up and following Dani.

Aaron didn't think he could feel any worse than he had before, but he was wrong.

Chapter 16

IN FRONT OF the center, Dani watched Levi get into his rental and waved goodbye to him. He would come back tomorrow to give the good news to Aaron, but Levi had refused to share that today. As far she knew, Aaron would be gone by then, but Levi said he had faith in his brother. He was an asshole, but he wasn't that big of one.

Dani didn't believe Levi. Not after what she'd seen and heard. The little boy in her heart was gone, and the man he had become was not somebody she wanted to spend any time around. Not any longer.

"Stay strong," Levi called out to her as he left.

That she could do. She had been doing that since forever. She returned to her office. At least she had a never-ending supply of work. About two hours later Stan called her.

"I think you should come down here," Stan said quietly. "It's Aaron."

He hung up before she had a chance to say anything. She stared at the phone in her hand for a long moment. She wanted to tell him she wasn't coming, but she had no choice. If Stan had called, then it was major.

Hating the nervous panic and worry forming in her stomach, she made her way to Stan's office. She stood in the doorway. "What's up?"

He motioned her to one of the rear treatment rooms.

"Go see for yourself."

She was about to refuse, but from the look in his eyes, she figured it was easier to take a peek. She walked down to the last treatment room and looked in through the window in the door. Aaron was busy fitting a new leg onto Helga, but the dog was having none of it. She was barking and running away excitedly as he tried to strap on the prosthesis. She didn't know why Aaron was in there all alone and not with Stan, but she assumed Aaron had a decent reason.

Stan stood beside her. "He's been designing new prostheses for her."

She nodded. "Good. Maybe that will be a career option for him in the future."

"Maybe." His voice was noncommittal. He nudged her arm. "Keep watching."

She studied Aaron again and saw when he caught the dog and held her close, he hugged her tight. When he let the wiggling bundle go, Dani caught a glimpse of his face, saw the tear tracks down his cheeks.

She closed her eyes and bowed her head. Was there anything like seeing a strong man cry to make her heart break?

"He told me an hour ago he was leaving. That everyone would be more than happy to see him gone." Stan sighed. "I don't know what's going on between the two of you, but I thought you should see this." He patted her shoulder and left.

Stan's words played on her mind. Yes, she would be happy to see Aaron go, only because having him here was a painful reminder of what she had lost. And he needed a stress-free environment to finish his healing. No matter how hurt she was, she wished him well.

She realized now how long she had cared for Aaron. She

closed her eyes. She prayed that it was a year later … so she didn't have to cope with this hurt, the pain … the loss. Opened her eyes. Saw Aaron with Helga. He smiled at the dog. But Dani still saw the hitch in his breathing.

She wished Aaron could somehow wipe away her agony. She almost laughed at the absurd thought. He was the one who had caused this agony.

She didn't think he had the words in him to mend her, to fix what he had broken.

Then she saw his face as he hugged Helga close again. His tears.

Maybe he did realize how much he had hurt Dani.

Maybe he was hurting, just like she was.

Maybe he wanted her to wipe away the agony he felt. Even knowing full well it was his fault.

Wanting love with no judgment.

Oh, my … Just like the animals give us.

Here she had been preaching about two-way charity and missing this deeper point. *Wow.*

Both of them had to get over this for any hope of a reconciliation to come about.

Some harsh words had been spoken. Hurtful words. Definitely something she never wanted to go through again.

Either way, she couldn't let Aaron leave like this. Not with so much anger and pain. Instead of knocking, she opened the door and stepped inside, closing it behind her. Helga raced toward Dani. She laughed and dropped to the floor beside Aaron, hugging the dancing dog. "You don't even need your spare, do you, girl? You just feel so free and unencumbered without the prosthesis. You're just happy to be alive and well."

"And to be loved."

She stiffened slightly at the pain in his voice. She nodded. "I think that's what we all want," she said quietly.

"Do you?" His tone was bitter. "I'm sure any number of people who want that would love a chance to love you."

"Apparently I don't want any of them," she said, tears choking her voice. "Seems I only like pigheaded, stubborn men."

"You're better off without those types."

This time she looked directly at him. "Maybe ... but don't count on that. Because I've liked this one *very stubborn* male for a long, long time."

His gaze was deep and fathomless. For a protracted moment, silence lay between them, as if neither knew what to do, what to say.

"I'm sorry."

She studied him carefully, looking into his eyes, searching for the truth—and finding it. She sighed. "I know you are. The thing is, that was your one shot. That was the one and only time you are allowed to blame me or hold me in any way accountable for the shit in your life. No more, do you hear me?"

A slow, tentative smile dawned on his face. "I was in pain, lashing out. I didn't mean what I said."

"You drew blood. Like I said, I'm not tolerating that anymore."

"Anymore? Does that mean you have forgiven me?" he asked, hope evident in his voice.

She looked at him for a long moment, then smiled. "I was afraid you'd react this way, right from the very beginning. I wanted to tell you, but Levi was adamant. For good reason," she added drily. "You just might be a tad sensitive on that issue."

He chuckled, then snaked an arm around her and pulled her close. "Thank you," he said against her ear. "You're a very warm, loving, generous soul."

"Don't you forget it," she said with spirit.

They sat on the cold hard floor in companionable silence for several long moments, just happy to no longer be at odds with each other. "I owe my brother an apology too."

She nodded. "You'll get the chance to tell him tomorrow morning."

He looked down at her. "He's coming back?"

"Yes. He has some good news for you but figured today wasn't the right day."

"If it's good news, I have no problem waiting," he said quietly, his tone one of acceptance. "Besides, if I get to hold you in my arms like this, I'm happy to wait forever." He dropped a kiss on her temple and just held her tight. "I still won't be a good bet for a long time, you know?"

"I wasn't asking for you to be a good bet," she said. "You have a lot of decisions to make moving forward. You have a lot of things to consider. I was just hoping to be one of the things you kept in your life."

His arms tightened around her. "If you have enough patience, give me a year, or maybe longer, to get back into a proper career. I have money. Not enough to pay for this treatment, but I do have money to keep myself going. I did speak with Stan about veterinary school, and I'm certainly considering it. This could be a five-year process."

She turned to look up at him, happy for him that he was considering such a move, and unintentionally repeated Stan's earlier question, "Were you planning on doing anything else in those five years?"

He looked down at her and smiled. "Maybe one thing

I'm hoping to do soon."

She frowned. "What's that?"

He dropped his head and said, "This."

He tentatively kissed her lips, as if testing the waters. Maybe it was too soon. But when she kissed him back without feeling hesitation or fear, he proceeded to kiss her passionately and thoroughly.

When he lifted his head, she said, "Yeah, we can do lots of that but not until the doctor clears you."

Aaron snickered. "I asked him a couple days ago."

"I'm sure he got a kick out of that." And Dani would never live it down. But it wasn't going to happen here. There were some lines that didn't need to be crossed. Not when she had a house of her own close by.

Aaron shook his head. "No, I think he was half expecting it." He fell silent again. "Do you think if I phoned Levi, he'd tell me?"

She studied his face and realized he had a lot riding on whatever Levi found out. No point in waiting. That was torture. She pulled out her phone and dialed Levi's number. When he answered, she said, "Your brother wants to speak with you." She handed the phone to Aaron.

HOLDING DANI CLOSE in his arms, Aaron took the phone. "I'm sorry, Levi. I had no business acting the way I did."

Levi said, "Good ... Glad that's over with."

Aaron laughed at his brother's evident surprise. "Well, not quite. I'm still groveling to get in Dani's good graces."

He dropped a kiss on her forehead.

"Keep groveling. That's one hell of a girl. You'd better

treat her right."

"I will," he promised. "She also said you had some good news for me, but you were coming back in the morning."

"I don't have to return in the morning," he said. "Now that your senses have returned, I'll tell you on the phone. We caught your buddy, on tape and over several beers, admitting to what he did."

Aaron froze and closed his eyes in relief. He'd wondered if this day would ever come.

Levi was still talking. "I've handed over the tape to the brass. They'll reopen the case and be in touch with you soon."

Aaron didn't know what to say. He choked out a simple, "Oh, thank God."

"Now think about what you'll say when they call. They owe you for this. You need to make sure you get something out of this."

"Like what?"

"Like money, for one. You don't want to owe me for your care? Then you can pay for the next man. If you need to get retraining, let the military pay. Don't enter into any conversations or negotiations without someone watching your back. Do you hear me?"

Aaron smiled. "I hear you, but I don't have anyone like that to help out."

"Yes, you do. Me." With that, Levi hung up.

Aaron slowly passed the phone to Dani and told her everything.

"Oh, that's fantastic! That should take a weight off your shoulders," she cried.

As he stared down at her, he realized how much his life had changed since he'd arrived here—and all because of her.

He realized another very simple truth.

He tilted her head up slightly and gazed into her huge chocolate-brown eyes. "I love you."

Her eyes widened, and a little gasp escaped.

"I wanted you back then too. But I wasn't the man you needed yet. It took this experience to grow me into the person you really need."

She threw her arms around his neck and hugged him close. Against his ear, she whispered, "I love you too." She pulled back slightly, tears coming to her eyes. "Since we were teenagers, you're all I've ever wanted." Dani kissed him, pouring her love and passion into that kiss.

Humbled, he could do no less than give it right back. Exactly as he'd always wanted to do.

"We have so much to talk about," he whispered in her ear. "I feel the need to prove myself to you after all this. I have ideas, plans, to run by you."

"Like what?" she asked. "I'd love to hear about them. You can tell me anything, you know?"

"I'll get better about communicating." He motioned to Helga, sensing their happiness and wagging her tag wildly, circling around the two of them, still sitting on the floor. "I'm good with animals. Not so good with people. But the only person I really need to share things with is you. So ..."

At his hesitation, she frowned. "Yes?"

"Here's what I've been thinking. I should probably finish my rehab here, and my team thinks I need another month ..."

Dani nodded, a big smile on her face.

"And no telling how long the navy will take to decide on the Cain matter ..."

At this Dani's eyebrows rose.

"But Levi thinks they owe me some money. Maybe between that and some educational grants I hope you might help me find …"

"Of course I'll help," she said.

"I want to be a veterinarian. And since A&M is so close, I was hoping to drive back and forth."

"You could take my car. It's an automatic. Plus maybe you could run some errands for me and the center while in town? You'd really be helping me out."

He kissed her on the nose. "You bet. I've got a little money saved, but it's not enough, so I'll barter my time for your vehicle. And, in that vein, I'd like to help Stan in the vet clinic and also you in the office—I *am* a bit of a computer geek—to offset my room and board, since I'll be staying long-term. That is, if it's okay with you?"

"Yes! This is so wonderful." She was in his lap, kissing him again.

He stopped to stare at her in wonder.

"What?" she asked.

"Who knew I'd end up here with you after all these years?"

Epilogue

Six Weeks Later ...

D ANI WALKED TO where Aaron sat on the fence. He still couldn't believe they were together. She was so damn special. And he'd been such a heel... Still he was strong and fit and looking forward to a future with her and hopefully going to veterinarian school.

He looked up and smiled, accepting the mug. "Midnight is enjoying being around the little one."

"Midnight loves everyone," she said with a chuckle. Then held out two pieces of mail.

He took a sip as he eyed the bigger envelope, from the DOD. He flashed it to her, and she nodded, patting his cheek this time. He opened it to find a licensing contract for his patent on Helga's special prosthesis. He showed Dani. "Sweetheart, I'm getting paid!"

She gasped and tried to focus on the document Aaron waved before her.

"I'm so proud of you, Aaron." She snuggled closer to him, dropping a kiss on his lips.

Then he saw the small number ten envelope with the navy's return address. He ripped it open, found the check and was speechless.

Dani raised her head. "What is it, honey?"

He held it before her eyes.

"Oh, my God."

He nodded. Looked at it again before he faced her. "I know exactly what to do with this. I want to use some of it for someone with no insurance or donation help to come to the center."

Tears came to Dani's eyes as she heard those words.

"And I want to choose who gets it. You've got four coming in a few days, right?"

She nodded, too choked up to speak.

"Any pro bono cases?"

"Yes, two," she said with a sniffle.

He smiled at her and kissed her forehead. "I'll let you know which one then." He waited as she reached for a tissue and blew her nose. "And one final piece of news."

She checked his hands, probably looking for more mail. Instead she saw the small jeweler's box. And gasped.

"Dani Hathaway," Aaron said, "you've been here for me during the worst of my days—and my out-of-control temper and ego. Now I want to spend the best of my days with you. Will you marry me?"

She was full-on crying now, hugging him close, trying to breathe through her mouth. And she was the most precious thing he had seen in his life. "Will you marry me, Dani?" he asked again.

She nodded, sniffling. "I've been waiting for you for most of my life."

THE FOUR NEWEST rehab patients arrived several weeks later, and Aaron and Dani—still staring at her engagement ring—were there to meet them. Along with George, Shane,

Dr. Herzog, the major, plus Helga, Racer, Tipler, Maggie and Molly. And so many more …

"Welcome to the Hathaway House," Aaron said, his arms spread wide. "We are all here to help in your healing and recovery. Yes even me…"

The four injured men seemed as dazed as Aaron probably was on his first day here. Then the three friends Dani was hoping to have in at the same time hadn't happened. Only one was here. But it was the one he knew. He perused the four and found him.

The first guy asked, "Where are we?"

"Texas," Aaron said with a smile.

The second guy took a 360-degree turn in his wheelchair, a blanket covering his lap but not hiding the fact he was missing a leg. He checked things out with a disapproving frown firmly in place. "You can't possibly know what I'm going through," he nearly growled.

Aaron raised his pant leg to show off his newest prosthesis. "Designed by yours truly."

The third guy was all stoic machismo silence, his one arm crossed tightly over his chest.

But it was the fourth man who asked, "What the hell is this place?"

Aaron whispered to Dani, "That's Brock. He's my guy." Then Aaron stepped forward to address all the newcomers as the words he was given on his first day came back to him. "Right now you hate this place. You want to be anywhere else but here. However, in a couple weeks, you'll never want to be anywhere else." He studied the men in front of him. "Are you ready?"

BROCK ONLY HALF listened to the conversation as he studied the man in front of him. A different man from the one he knew. Then major trauma changed a person. He didn't know the first thing about this place. And maybe that was a good thing. Maybe—if they also didn't know about him— he could start fresh.

Brock knew Aaron. Not well like many others he knew, but Aaron was a good man. A solid fighter and someone Brock could trust. If Aaron had done okay here, then maybe ... And if that was the case then the rest of Brock's unit could also come. Cole, Denton, Elliot—had all been injured in a mission after Brock had been hospitalized. Brock knew Elliot the best. But doubted he'd like Hathaway House. Not his style.

Then again, Brock's unit had all changed. Who knew what lay ahead of them? What he did know was there was no going back. This was his life now—no matter how he felt about it. So far it had been ugly as sin.

He waited a moment, then gave a decisive nod. "Let's do it."

This concludes Book 1 of Hathaway House: Aaron.
Read about Brock: Hathaway House, Book 2

Welcome to Hathaway House. Rehab Center. Safe Haven. Second chance at life and love.

Former Navy SEAL Brock Gorman has been at Hathaway House for more than a month with minimal improvement to either his physical or mental health. An vehicle accident on base two months ago caused major hip, back, and shoulder injuries that and took away any chance he had of ever going on a mission again. Making it through BUD/S training and into the SEALs teams was the crowning glory of Brock's life. Now it's gone. Why try to get better when he has nothing left to live for?

Physiotherapist Sidney Morning has been away from Hathaway House for nine months of specialized training. When she returns, there's Brock. And, while she loves the tough cases, he might be more than she can handle. He's big. He's strong. He's stubborn. He's gorgeous. And he's not making the efforts needed to get better. But, if Sidney can get under his skin and force him to jumping hurdles he's not interested in jumping, she can help him see that there are things which still make life worth living.

Sparks fly as Sidney and Brock fight their own emotions and each other, pushing Brock where he needs to go. ... If they are lucky, he might find both healing and love at Hathaway House.

Book 2 is available now!

To find out more visit Dale Mayer's website.

http://smarturl.it/BrockDMUniversal

Author's Note

Thank you for reading Aaron: Hathaway House, Book 1! If you enjoyed the book, please take a moment and leave a short review.

Dear reader,

I love to hear from readers, and you can contact me at my website: www.dalemayer.com or at my Facebook author page. To be informed of new releases and special offers, sign up for my newsletter or follow me on BookBub. And if you are interested in joining Dale Mayer's Reader Group, here is the Facebook sign up page.
facebook.com/groups/402384989872660

Cheers,
Dale Mayer

Get THREE Free Books Now!

Have you met the SEALS of Honor?

SEALs of Honor Books 1, 2, and 3. Follow the stories of brave, badass warriors who serve their country with honor and love their women to the limits of life and death.

Read Mason, Hawk, and Dane right now for FREE.

Go here and tell me where to send them!
http://smarturl.it/EthanBofB

About the Author

Dale Mayer is a USA Today bestselling author best known for her Psychic Visions and Family Blood Ties series. Her contemporary romances are raw and full of passion and emotion (Second Chances, SKIN), her thrillers will keep you guessing (By Death series), and her romantic comedies will keep you giggling (It's a Dog's Life and Charmin Marvin Romantic Comedy series).

She honors the stories that come to her – and some of them are crazy and break all the rules and cross multiple genres!

To go with her fiction, she also writes nonfiction in many different fields with books available on resume writing, companion gardening and the US mortgage system. She has recently published her Career Essentials Series. All her books are available in print and ebook format.

Connect with Dale Mayer Online

Dale's Website – www.dalemayer.com
Twitter – @DaleMayer
Facebook – dalemayer.com/fb
BookBub – bookbub.com/authors/dale-mayer

Also by Dale Mayer

Published Adult Books:

Hathaway House
Aaron, Book 1
Brock, Book 2

The K9 Files
Ethan, Book 1
Pierce, Book 2
Zane, Book 3
Blaze, Book 4
Lucas, Book 5
Parker, Book 6
Carter, Book 7

Lovely Lethal Gardens
Arsenic in the Azaleas, Book 1
Bones in the Begonias, Book 2
Corpse in the Carnations, Book 3
Daggers in the Dahlias, Book 4
Evidence in the Echinacea, Book 5
Footprints in the Ferns, Book 6

Psychic Vision Series
Tuesday's Child
Hide 'n Go Seek
Maddy's Floor

Garden of Sorrow
Knock Knock...
Rare Find
Eyes to the Soul
Now You See Her
Shattered
Into the Abyss
Seeds of Malice
Eye of the Falcon
Itsy-Bitsy Spider
Unmasked
Deep Beneath
From the Ashes
Psychic Visions Books 1–3
Psychic Visions Books 4–6
Psychic Visions Books 7–9

By Death Series
Touched by Death
Haunted by Death
Chilled by Death
By Death Books 1–3

Broken Protocols – Romantic Comedy Series
Cat's Meow
Cat's Pajamas
Cat's Cradle
Cat's Claus
Broken Protocols 1-4

Broken and... Mending
Skin
Scars

Scales (of Justice)
Broken but... Mending 1-3

Glory
Genesis
Tori
Celeste
Glory Trilogy

Biker Blues
Morgan: Biker Blues, Volume 1
Cash: Biker Blues, Volume 2

SEALs of Honor
Mason: SEALs of Honor, Book 1
Hawk: SEALs of Honor, Book 2
Dane: SEALs of Honor, Book 3
Swede: SEALs of Honor, Book 4
Shadow: SEALs of Honor, Book 5
Cooper: SEALs of Honor, Book 6
Markus: SEALs of Honor, Book 7
Evan: SEALs of Honor, Book 8
Mason's Wish: SEALs of Honor, Book 9
Chase: SEALs of Honor, Book 10
Brett: SEALs of Honor, Book 11
Devlin: SEALs of Honor, Book 12
Easton: SEALs of Honor, Book 13
Ryder: SEALs of Honor, Book 14
Macklin: SEALs of Honor, Book 15
Corey: SEALs of Honor, Book 16
Warrick: SEALs of Honor, Book 17
Tanner: SEALs of Honor, Book 18
Jackson: SEALs of Honor, Book 19

Kanen: SEALs of Honor, Book 20
Nelson: SEALs of Honor, Book 21
SEALs of Honor, Books 1–3
SEALs of Honor, Books 4–6
SEALs of Honor, Books 7–10
SEALs of Honor, Books 11–13
SEALs of Honor, Books 14–16
SEALs of Honor, Books 17–19

Heroes for Hire
Levi's Legend: Heroes for Hire, Book 1
Stone's Surrender: Heroes for Hire, Book 2
Merk's Mistake: Heroes for Hire, Book 3
Rhodes's Reward: Heroes for Hire, Book 4
Flynn's Firecracker: Heroes for Hire, Book 5
Logan's Light: Heroes for Hire, Book 6
Harrison's Heart: Heroes for Hire, Book 7
Saul's Sweetheart: Heroes for Hire, Book 8
Dakota's Delight: Heroes for Hire, Book 9
Michael's Mercy (Part of Sleeper SEAL Series)
Tyson's Treasure: Heroes for Hire, Book 10
Jace's Jewel: Heroes for Hire, Book 11
Rory's Rose: Heroes for Hire, Book 12
Brandon's Bliss: Heroes for Hire, Book 13
Liam's Lily: Heroes for Hire, Book 14
North's Nikki: Heroes for Hire, Book 15
Anders's Angel: Heroes for Hire, Book 16
Reyes's Raina: Heroes for Hire, Book 17
Dezi's Diamond: Heroes for Hire, Book 18
Vince's Vixen: Heroes for Hire, Book 19
Heroes for Hire, Books 1–3
Heroes for Hire, Books 4–6

Heroes for Hire, Books 7–9
Heroes for Hire, Books 10–12
Heroes for Hire, Books 13–15

SEALs of Steel
Badger: SEALs of Steel, Book 1
Erick: SEALs of Steel, Book 2
Cade: SEALs of Steel, Book 3
Talon: SEALs of Steel, Book 4
Laszlo: SEALs of Steel, Book 5
Geir: SEALs of Steel, Book 6
Jager: SEALs of Steel, Book 7
The Final Reveal: SEALs of Steel, Book 8
SEALs of Steel, Books 1–4
SEALs of Steel, Books 5–8
SEALs of Steel, Books 1–8

Collections
Dare to Be You…
Dare to Love…
Dare to be Strong…
RomanceX3

Standalone Novellas
It's a Dog's Life
Riana's Revenge
Second Chances

Published Young Adult Books:

Family Blood Ties Series
Vampire in Denial
Vampire in Distress

Vampire in Design
Vampire in Deceit
Vampire in Defiance
Vampire in Conflict
Vampire in Chaos
Vampire in Crisis
Vampire in Control
Vampire in Charge
Family Blood Ties Set 1–3
Family Blood Ties Set 1–5
Family Blood Ties Set 4–6
Family Blood Ties Set 7–9
Sian's Solution, A Family Blood Ties Series Prequel
    Novelette

Design series
Dangerous Designs
Deadly Designs
Darkest Designs
Design Series Trilogy

Standalone
In Cassie's Corner
Gem Stone (a Gemma Stone Mystery)
Time Thieves

Published Non-Fiction Books:

Career Essentials
Career Essentials: The Résumé
Career Essentials: The Cover Letter
Career Essentials: The Interview
Career Essentials: 3 in 1

CPSIA information can be obtained
at www.ICGtesting.com
Printed in the USA
LVHW031518021019
632974LV00010B/753/P